THEY DIDN'T EVEN
HAVE A CHANCE...

"Let me ask you something before the shooting starts," Clint said.

"What?"

"Were you hired to do this," Clint asked, "or is it your own stupid idea?"

Roy went for his gun, bringing the whole conversation to a halt in a hail of gunfire. When it was over, the three men were lying in the street and Clint was untouched. So was the girl behind him.

So were the guns of the three men, which were still snugly in their holsters.

THE GUNSMITH

194

MASSACRE AT ROCK SPRINGS

J. R. ROBERTS

JOVE BOOKS, NEW YORK

MASSACRE AT ROCK SPRINGS

A Jove Book / published by arrangement with
the author

PRINTING HISTORY
Jove edition / March 1998

All rights reserved.
Copyright © 1998 by Robert J. Randisi.
This book may not be reproduced in whole
or in part, by mimeograph or any other means,
without permission. For information address:
The Berkley Publishing Group, a member of Penguin Putnam Inc.,
200 Madison Avenue, New York, New York 10016.

The Penguin Putnam Inc. World Wide Web site address is
http://www.penguinputnam.com

ISBN: 0-515-12245-9

A JOVE BOOK®
Jove Books are published by The Berkley Publishing Group,
a member of Penguin Putnam Inc.,
200 Madison Avenue, New York, New York 10016.
JOVE and the "J" design are trademarks
belonging to Jove Publications, Inc.

PRINTED IN THE UNITED STATES OF AMERICA

10 9 8 7 6 5 4 3 2 1

THE GUNSMITH

194

MASSACRE AT ROCK SPRINGS

PROLOGUE

Rock Springs, Wyoming

Sam Crider looked out the front window of his office. Outside, just above his head, was a sign that said ROCK SPRINGS MINING DEVELOPMENT COMPANY. Behind him, sitting in his chair behind his desk, was his partner, Rod Craig. Crider didn't have to turn around to know that Craig had a chart spread out over his desk and was frowning over it. Craig was the half of the operation who had the nose for coal. He was rarely wrong when he picked a new direction in which to dig into a mountain. Invariably, they struck another vein of coal. Sometimes Crider didn't know why Craig even needed him as a partner. He had no nose for coal and, for another thing, he was the eternal pessimist.

Finally, he turned and saw his partner hunched over his desk, just as he had seen him in his mind's eye.

"I don't know why you're doing that," he said. "If these men strike there's going to be no one to dig the ore out of the ground."

Craig looked up from the chart and locked eyes with his partner. Both men were in their late thirties, but Craig looked older. He had a craggy, pockmarked face that he tried to hide with a bushy black beard. Crider had a smooth face, a handsome one, if the women who told him so were to be believed.

"That's your end of the business, Sam," Craig said.

1

"You're the one who's good with people. If we had to rely on me to negotiate we'd never get any coal out of the ground."

"I've got a meeting tonight that might help us out of this mess, Rod," Crider said, "but I'm not holding my breath."

"That's okay, Sam," Craig said, shaking his head, "if you were optimistic, then I'd be worried."

With that Craig turned his attention back to his work, and Crider turned and continued to look out the window.

Hours later Crider was grunting over the writhing form of Virginia Madison. While his partner, Craig, frequented the whorehouse in town and had a different woman every night, Crider had used the past six months to form a relationship with Virginia. Lately, however, the relationship had consisted largely of hurried sex each evening.

"Slow down . . ." he said.

"Come on, come on," she implored him. Her nails dug into his naked ass as she pulled him to her.

"I want to go slower . . ."

"Faster," she said, shaking her head from side to side so violently that sweat leapt from her brow. Her long, dark hair appeared even darker where it was plastered to her head by her perspiration—and his, which was dripping down from his chin onto her.

Her breasts, large and firm, were slick and slippery beneath him. If it weren't for her insistence on going fast they wouldn't be building up this much of a sweat. . . .

Oh, what the hell, he thought, he had to get to a meeting soon, anyway.

He quickened his pace, gave her what she wanted, and soon they were both grunting until finally he shouted and spurted into her. She began to buck beneath him in a mindless dance that ended their violent and only mildly satisfying coupling. . . .

"You could stay," she said, lying on her belly and watching him dress. "We could do it again."

"I have to go," he said, "but I could come back later."

"Don't bother," she said, turning on her back. Her breasts barely flattened out they were so firm. "Later I'll be asleep."

He wondered if that was the truth, or would someone else be here in her bed later? Should he ask her? No, she'd give him the same answer she always did, that he was paranoid.

"All right, then," he said, tucking his shirt into his pants. "I'll see you tomorrow."

"All right," she said, wiping sweat from her brow with the back of her wrist. "Maybe it won't be this hot tomorrow."

They both knew that wouldn't be true. It was September, but it still felt like the middle of summer.

"Maybe not," he said. "Goodnight, Virginia."

"Night, Sam."

He wasn't out the door when he heard her deep, even breathing. Was she really asleep or faking? He shook his head, dispelling thoughts of her with another man— or trying to—and reminding himself that he had business to conduct tonight—serious business.

He was going to meet with someone who said he could help Crider and Craig head off a strike by the coal miners. A strike they could not afford to have. Crider had tried everything he knew during negotiations, but nothing had worked. Maybe this man would, indeed, have an idea.

If not, Crider was seriously thinking about returning

to the East and giving up on making his fortune in the West.

The dead man lay on the office floor of the Rock Springs Mining Development Company. He was bleeding heavily from the head, which had been bashed open as he entered the office. The killer crossed the room to the safe, left ajar. He opened it, reached inside, and removed whatever money he found there. He left the safe door open, then crossed the room, stepping over the body, being careful not to step in the blood. The last thing he wanted was to leave bloody footprints behind him.

He looked down at the man on the floor again, feeling nothing. Killing him had been a necessity, one that he swore he would not regret. He looked around the room, then opened the door, peered out, and left, closing the door behind him.

Moments later there was a knock at the door, then another, and then it opened. This time the man who stepped inside made no attempt to avoid the blood, because he did not know it was there. He slipped on it, then fell heavily, getting blood all over his clothes.

Which was the bulk of the evidence that would be used against him later on.

ONE

On the day Clint rode into Rock Springs the heat had broken. Although he had a fine sheen of sweat on his forehead, the breeze was cool against it and he did not feel uncomfortable at all.

Rock Springs had grown by leaps and bounds since the last time he was there. Just six months earlier, when his friends had started their business, there had only been a few shacks and a lot of tents. Now the tents were mostly gone, except for the ones being used to house some of the miners. Everywhere else, however, new wood buildings had gone up. There was a saloon, a livery, and, thankfully, a hotel. Clint rode to the livery first, then walked to the hotel, and finally made it to the saloon.

"Passin' through?" the bartender asked, while serving him a cold beer.

"No," Clint said. "Came to see a couple of friends."

"Might be I know them," the barkeep said, settling his beefy elbows on the bar. "Who might they be?"

"Crider and Craig?" Clint said. "The Rock Springs Mining Company, or whatever they call it."

The man stood straight up.

"Say, then you ain't heard?"

"Heard what?" Clint asked, sipping the beer.

"About the killin'?"

5

Clint wiped his mouth with the back of his hand.

"What killin'?"

"Sam Crider."

"Sam killed somebody?"

"No," the bartender said, "he went and got hisself killed."

Clint put his beer down.

"When was this?"

"Just a few days ago."

"Did they get who did it?"

"They sure did."

"Who was it?"

"A goddamned Chinaman."

"Is that a fact?"

"Caught him almost red-handed," the bartender said. "Well, actually, he *was* kinda red-handed, and red-footed, he had red all over him."

"What do you mean?"

"He bashed poor Sam's head in, and then got the blood all over him."

"Where is he?"

"They got him over at the jail."

"And where's Craig?"

"He's around. He's all broke up over it."

"Damn it," Clint said. He took one more sip of the beer and then slammed it down on the bar.

"Was you good friends with Sam?" the bartender asked.

"Yeah," Clint said. "All three of us were good friends."

"Well, I tell you what, then," the bartender said. "I ain't gonna charge you for the beer, in honor of ol' Sam."

"Thanks," Clint said, "thanks a lot."

He left the saloon and headed over to the office of the mining company he had helped build.

TWO

When Clint entered the office of the Rock Springs Mining Development Company, Rod Craig looked up from his desk.

"Clint!" he said, getting to his feet.

Clint crossed the room and the two men shook hands.

"I just heard about Sam," Clint said.

"Jesus," Craig said, sitting heavily in his chair and passing a hand over his face. "Can you believe it?"

"Who's this fella they say killed him?"

"His name's Lee To."

"Did he have a fight with Sam?"

"Not beforehand."

"Then why do you think he killed him?"

"I don't know, Clint," Craig said. "You're gonna have to talk to the sheriff."

"Last time I was here there was no sheriff."

"Last time you were here there was no town," Craig said. "Now there is, and we hired a sheriff."

"You did," Clint asked "or the town?"

"He's paid by the town," Craig said, "but Sam and I picked him out. His name's Cody Reasoner. We hired him three months ago, and built him a new jail."

"I never heard of him."

"He's young, not yet thirty," Craig said. "This is his

first time wearing a sheriff's star, but he's been deputying since he was eighteen.''

"You mind if I talk to him?'' Clint asked.

"No, I don't mind,'' Craig said. "You're still a partner in this company.''

"Investor,'' Clint corrected him.

"Whatever,'' Craig said. "Jesus, I can't believe Sam's dead.''

"Rod,'' Clint said, "how's the business doing?''

"The truth?'' Craig asked. "Not good.''

"I thought you had rich deposits of coal ore—''

"Oh, the ore is there,'' Craig said.

"Then what's the problem?''

"Diggin' it out,'' Craig said. "The miners are talkin' about a strike. If they do that we're gonna fall behind, and we won't be able to make our next loan payment in time.''

"Why do they want to strike?''

"Beats me,'' Craig said. "Sam was handling that. He did all our negotiating with the men, with the bank, with everybody.''

Clint knew that Crider and Craig had very definitely split their duties up. It was one of the reasons he'd decided, six months ago, to invest in the venture when they first approached him about it. He had met them in Rock Springs and they had laid the whole business out for him.

"And we have another problem,'' Craig said.

"What's that?''

"The Chinese.''

"What about them?''

"The men don't want to work with them.''

"Because one of them killed Sam?'' Clint asked.

"No, this was before that. There's been tension between them since we brought the Chinese in.''

"Sam was handling that, too?''

Craig nodded. "But there's more."

"Let me have all of it."

"If the men are really going to strike, we were going to bring in more Chinese."

"How many more?"

Craig hesitated, then said, "Hundreds."

Clint whistled.

"We'd need them to get the work done, Clint."

"The strikers wouldn't like that," Clint said. "That would bring real trouble."

"That's what we hired a sheriff for," Craig said.

"Okay, Rod," Clint said. "I'm going to talk to the sheriff and then I'll meet you back here. We can get some dinner and talk some more."

"That's fine with me," Craig said. He shook hands with Clint again. "I'm really glad you're here."

THREE

Clint knocked on the door of the brand-new sheriff's office and entered. The inside still smelled like new wood, and it would be a while before it acquired the same smells as most jails had—sweat, gun oil, and coffee.

"Can I help you?"

A man behind a desk stood, and Clint saw the sheriff's star on his chest.

"Sheriff Reasoner?"

"That's right."

Reasoner was a big man, especially big above the waist, lots of chest and belly, but he carried it well. He looked more like a powerful man than a fat man.

"My name's Clint Adams."

Reasoner's face brightened.

"I know who you are, Mr. Adams. What can I do for you? What brings you to Rock Springs?"

"I *was* coming here to see a couple of friends, but I heard one of them got killed."

"You're friends with Mr. Craig and Mr. Crider?"

"That's right," Clint said. "I'm also an investor in their company."

"Well, hearing about Mr. Crider must have been a real shock to you." Reasoner sat back down behind his desk.

"Yes, it was," Clint said. "I understand you have a suspect in your jail?"

"Oh, he ain't just a suspect," the sheriff said. "He did it."

"Has he confessed?"

"No," Reasoner said, "but he did it."

"Is he going to stand trial?"

"He sure is," the lawman said, "just as soon as the judge gets to town."

"And when will that be?"

Reasoner shrugged and said, "A week, maybe two."

"And you're going to keep him here the whole time?"

"Sure."

"Do you have any deputies?"

" 'Fraid not."

"Then who'll be guarding the prisoner when you're out of the office?"

"Guarding?" Reasoner asked. "Why would he have to be guarded? He ain't gonna get away."

"I wasn't thinking of him getting away," Clint said. "I was thinking more along the lines of him getting killed."

"You think some of Mr. Crider's friends will try to kill him?"

"If they get drunk enough." Clint refused to believe that Sheriff Reasoner hadn't thought of that himself. It was more likely that the man didn't care. Maybe he thought it would just be fitting mining town justice.

"Sheriff," Clint said, "maybe it's none of my business—"

"If you were Mr. Crider's friend," Reasoner said, cutting him off, "and an investor, then I'd say it sure was your business."

"Okay, then," Clint said, "I can say what I want to say."

"Go ahead."

"You can't let that man get killed before he has a fair trial."

Reasoner frowned.

"Everybody in town knows he did it," he said. "I'd think you'd want him punished."

"If he did it, I *do* want him punished, but by a court of law."

"And he will be," Reasoner said, "as soon as the judge gets here."

"If he's still alive."

"Well," Reasoner said, "there is that."

Now it was Clint's turn to frown. "Can I see him?"

"Who?"

"The prisoner," Clint said. "I'd like to talk to him."

"What for?"

"Does he speak English?"

"He speaks English, all right," Reasoner said. "He can say 'I no kill Mr. Clider.' " Reasoner's Oriental mimicry was awful.

"Then I'd like to talk to him, please."

"Why?"

"I'd just like to satisfy myself about his guilt or innocence."

"And you think you can do that by talking to him?"

"Yes, I do."

Reasoner leaned back in his chair, sighed, then stood up and plucked the key off of a peg on the wall.

"Come on," he said.

Clint followed the lawman into the back, where the cells were. Only one was inhabited. The Chinese man was sitting cross-legged on the cot, looking very relaxed.

"You got a visitor, Chinaman," Reasoner said.

"Can I go inside the cell?" Clint asked.

"That's why I brought the key," Reasoner said. "I

figure if you're gonna read his mind you're gonna have to get close to him.''

Reasoner opened the cell door. Clint stepped in, and the lawman closed it and locked it behind him.

''Sing out when you're finished,'' Reasoner said, ''and I'll come and let you out.''

With that he left Clint and the Chinese prisoner alone together.

FOUR

"Can you speak English?" Clint asked.

The man nodded. He didn't look like any Chinese Clint had ever seen. For one thing his hair wasn't black, it was more brown. And his eyes weren't as slanted as most Chinese Clint had met.

"Are you half Chinese?" Clint asked.

The man nodded.

"My mother was white." He spoke in very slow, measured tones.

"Ah, that would explain your hair."

The man touched his hair with one hand at the mention of it.

"It is the color of my mother's."

"Is your mother still alive?"

"No."

"Your father?"

"No."

"Your name is Lee, right?"

A nod.

"Lee To?"

Another nod.

"Lee, did you kill Sam Crider?"

"I did not."

"But everyone says you did."

Lee To shrugged and said again, "I did not."

15

"You were covered with his blood."

"I fell."

"Did you trip over him?"

"My foot slipped on the blood," he said, "and I fell."

"Lee, what were you doing at the mining office that late at night?"

"I was out walking," Lee said. "I saw Mr. Sam go into the office. I wanted to talk to him."

"About what?"

"About the strike."

"What about it?"

"I wanted to tell him that my people were prepared to work if the miners went on strike."

"Wouldn't that be dangerous for you and your people?" Clint asked.

Lee shrugged.

"We must work."

"So you went into the office to talk to him and slipped on his blood. You fell, and that's how you got his blood all over you. Is that your story?"

"Yes."

It made sense to Clint. That is, it certainly could have happened that way.

"Lee," Clint said, "would you have had any reason to kill Sam Crider?"

"None."

"Can I ask why you seem so calm?"

"I am to go on trial, am I not?"

"That's right."

"I will be found innocent."

"How do you know?"

"Is it not true in this country that the innocent need not fear justice?"

"It's *supposed* to be true, yes."

Again that very eloquent shrug of his shoulders.

"I am innocent. I will be found innocent and set free."

"If you're innocent like you say," Clint asked, "did you see anyone else there that night?"

"No."

"There was no other man there?"

"I did not say that," Lee answered. "I said I did not see anyone else."

Clint supposed that if there was another man there that night he might have already been in the office, waiting.

"The safe was robbed," Lee said.

"It was?"

Lee nodded.

"And did they find any money on you?"

"No."

No one had told Clint that. Looking into the utter calm of Lee To's eyes, Clint couldn't help but believe the man.

"You believe me," Lee To said, as if he'd read Clint's mind.

"Yes."

"Then I have nothing to fear."

"Not from me," Clint said, but convincing Clint of his innocence was the least of Lee To's worries.

FIVE

"He what?" Reasoner asked.

"He didn't do it."

"He told you that, did he?" Reasoner looked up at Clint from behind his desk.

"Yes."

"And you believe him?"

"I do, yes."

"Well . . ." Reasoner said.

"Where was the money?"

"What?"

"The money that was stolen from the safe," Clint said. "Where was it?"

"I don't know."

"Did he have it on him when you found him?"

"Well, no . . ."

"Then where is it?"

"Maybe he had an accomplice," the sheriff said, "or maybe he hid it."

"Where? In the office?"

"Outside."

"Did you look for it?"

"Well . . . yeah . . ."

"And you didn't find it?"

"No."

Clint shook his head.

"Why do you believe him?" Reasoner asked.

"That's a tough question to answer," Clint said. "It's in his eyes."

"His eyes?"

Clint nodded.

"He's too calm," Clint said. "He's too willing to trust a court of law to find him innocent—because he is innocent. If he was guilty, he'd be worried."

"Maybe he is worried," Reasoner said, "and he just ain't showing it."

"I don't think so."

"Well," Reasoner said, "it's too bad for the China-man you don't live here in Rock Springs, Mr. Adams."

"Why's that?"

"You can't sit on his jury."

"He what?" Rod Craig said.

"He didn't do it."

"How can you say that?"

"How can you say he did?"

"He was covered with Sam's blood."

"He explained that."

"And you believed him?"

"It makes sense, Rod."

"Ah!" Craig erupted. "I'll tell you what makes sense. He had Sam's blood on him because he killed him."

"Why would he kill him?"

"Because Sam caught him going through the safe, that's why."

"If that's the case, where's the money?"

"He hid it."

"The way I understand it," Clint said, "the sheriff got there pretty quick."

"So?"

"So where would he have hidden it? He wouldn't have had time."

"Maybe he gave it to an accomplice."

Craig was making all the same arguments that the sheriff had.

"Maybe . . ."

"Look," Craig said, "he's gonna have a trial when the judge gets here."

"If he's still alive."

"Meaning what?"

"Meaning the sheriff is going to be leaving him alone in his cell from time to time," Clint said. "Like when he goes to dinner. That'd be plenty of time for someone to slip in and kill him."

"Why?"

"For revenge."

"You think I'd do that?"

"Not you," Clint said, "but Sam had other friends in town, didn't he?"

"I suppose."

"And men who were loyal to him?"

"Well, sure . . ."

"And the sheriff has no deputies."

"Why are you so all-fired willing to believe this Chinaman?" Craig demanded.

"Why are you so ready to condemn him?"

"Because of the evidence."

"What evidence?" Clint asked. "There was no money, and no weapon, right?"

"There's the blood."

"And he explained that. You and I know how slippery blood is, Rod."

"You're damned right I know," Craig said. "Who do you think had to clean my partner's blood off the floor of this office?"

He was seated behind his desk, but he pointed to

where Crider had been found. Clint looked and saw that not all of the blood had come up off the wooden floor. Some of it had soaked in and would probably be there for a long time.

"I'm sorry as hell about Sam, Rod," Clint said, "but I just don't think Lee killed him."

"Well, luckily, that's what we have courts for."

Yeah, Clint thought, if he gets to court.

SIX

Clint understood the anger that Rod Craig had toward him. After all, Craig was convinced that Lee To had killed his partner. The question Clint had to answer now was, if Lee didn't kill Sam Crider, who did?

Two men faced each other at the mouth of the abandoned mine shaft.

"Adams doesn't believe that Lee To killed Crider," the first man said.

"That's just what we didn't need," the second man said.

"Who invited him?"

"Actually, Crider did. Did you have to kill him? You could have held off—"

"*You* didn't tell me that Adams was coming," the second man said, "but I don't think it would have mattered. Crider had to go, no matter what."

"Adams isn't going to go away," the first man said. "If he believes that Crider's killer is still free he'll look for him."

"For me, you mean."

"And he won't allow that Chinaman to pay for it."

"He won't have a choice," the second man said. "The Chinaman is going to die before any judge gets here."

"You better do it, then."

"Oh, I will," the second man said, "but it's going to cost extra."

"Don't worry about that," Rod Craig said to the second man. "Now that I don't have to share the profits with Sam Crider it won't be a problem to pay you."

"What about the strike?"

"I'll handle the strikers," Craig said.

"I thought Crider was the one who handled people?"

"Well," Craig said, "he's not around anymore to do it, is he?"

"I'm curious," the second man said.

"About what?"

"About how it feels to hire somebody to kill your friend?"

"Friendship is one thing," Craig said, "and business is another. Crider was holding me back."

"Well," the second man said, "there's nothing holding you back anymore, is there?"

"Only Clint Adams."

"And I'm going to take care of that little problem for you," the second man said, "just like I always do."

SEVEN

Clint went back to the hotel to do some thinking. It didn't seem likely that Craig was going to help him find a killer other than Lee To. That meant that he was going to have to find someone in town who could fill him in on what had been going on for the past six months in Rock Springs.

He thought about Virginia Madison.

When Clint had first come to Rock Springs, Virginia Madison had not yet been Crider's woman. That had happened after he left. Before he left, though, he and Virginia had spent some time together. Maybe she could help him answer some questions.

The only other person Clint could think to talk to was the bartender in the saloon. Bartenders were always talkative.

And then there was Jeff Banks.

Banks ramroded the mining operation for Crider and Craig. He was the one who actually got down in the mines with the men, something Crider rarely did, and Craig *never* did—which was probably the reason the men liked Crider more than his partner. At least he actually went down in a mine once in a while.

Clint had thought about seeing Virginia when he came to Rock Springs, but he thought he'd be seeing her as Sam Crider's woman. That might have been awkward,

25

but their relationship would have been defined.

Would their meeting now be more awkward and their relationship less defined?

He decided to find out right away.

Virginia Madison had her own house. It was at the far southern end of town, and in fact was not technically within the town's city limits. Still it was an easy walk from Clint's hotel.

Virginia had had the house six months ago when Clint was there, but she was thinking of leaving because it looked to her like Rock Springs as a town was never going to happen. Sam Crider and Rod Craig changed that. Clint had been in touch with Crider a few times over the past six months. Actually, that wasn't true. He had *heard* from Crider over that time, and in one letter Crider had told him of the developing relationship with Virginia Madison. Clint did not know how far that relationship had developed, but he supposed he was about to find out.

The small house looked much better than it had the last time he saw it. He knew that it had a living room, a kitchen, and one bedroom. It was small and well kept, while the last time he had seen it, it had been in a state of some disrepair.

He mounted the small porch and knocked on the door. When Virginia answered the door he recognized her immediately, although she had changed somewhat. Six months had passed, but she seemed years older to him. Those supposed years, however, seemed to have added to her beauty, maturing it. Her long dark hair was worn loose, the way he remembered it. Her skin was pale, her body full, more womanly than he remembered. He knew she was about twenty-five, but she seemed older.

"Clint?"

"Hello, Virginia."

"Clint Adams," she said, swinging the door open. She stepped out and embraced him. It started out as a sisterly embrace, but when she pressed her body to his she didn't feel like a sister to him. They embraced briefly and then she stepped back, appearing embarrassed.

"When did you get to town?"

"Just today."

"Have you, uh, heard about Sam?"

"Yes."

"Come inside," she said. "I'll put some coffee on."

"All right."

She led him into the house, through the small living room into the kitchen.

"Sit down," she said. "I remember you like your coffee strong."

"Yes," he said. That brought back to him the memory of when he had told her that. They were in bed.

He watched as she moved around the kitchen, preparing the coffee.

"Something to eat?"

"No," he said. "I really came to talk, Virginia."

"Talk?" She seemed nervous suddenly. "Talk about what?"

"Sam, and what happened to him."

She turned to face him, her back up against the stove.

"What if I don't want to talk about that, Clint?"

"I need you to."

"Why?"

"Because I think they've got the wrong man in jail."

She looked at him strangely. "You said you just got here today?"

"I did."

"And already you think you know who didn't kill him?" she asked. "They have evidence."

"They have no evidence," Clint said. "Lee To said he slipped on the blood and fell into it. That's a perfectly logical explanation of how he came to have Sam's blood on him.''

"What was he doing there at that time of night?"

"He said he wanted to talk to Sam about the possible miners' strike."

"Maybe they argued."

"They say money was stolen from the safe," Clint said. "Where is it?"

"He didn't have it?"

"No."

"Maybe he hid it."

"Even if he had time, it hasn't been found."

She came to the table with the coffeepot and two cups. She was thoughtful as she poured them full and then sat down.

"I didn't know any of this," she said. "I thought he did it."

"He may have," Clint said, "but I don't think so."

"Then who do you think did it?"

"Now that," he said, "I haven't been here long enough to guess at."

They sipped their coffee during an awkward, silent moment.

"Who do *you* think might have done it, if Lee To didn't, Virginia?"

She laughed nervously.

"I knew you were going to ask me that."

"Do you have an answer?"

"Not one that you'd like."

"Why don't you let me hear it?"

She hesitated, rubbed at the back of her neck for a moment, then started worrying a strand of hair.

"Craig," she said, finally, "I think Rod Craig might have had reason to kill Sam."

EIGHT

"Why Rod?"

"Some things that Sam had been saying lately," she said. "He and Rod weren't getting along too well."

"Why not?"

"They were arguing about this possible strike," she said. "Sam wanted to give in to some of the miners' demands, and Rod didn't. Rod wanted to bring in the Chinese workers, and Sam didn't. Things like that."

"What about you?" Clint asked.

"What about me?"

"Were they fighting over you?"

"Why would they?"

"When I left, Virginia," he said, "I knew you'd end up with one of them, I just didn't know which one. They both wanted you."

"Yes," she said, almost wistfully, "yes, they did."

"And you ended up with Sam."

"Yes, I did," she said, not sounding so wistful.

"Were you and Sam . . . having problems, too?"

"I guess that would depend on who you asked," she said.

"Were you having problems?"

"He didn't think so," she said. "Everything was fine to him. He'd come here in the evenings, we'd go to bed, and then he'd go back to work."

"And you wanted more?"

"Much more."

"Marriage?"

She bit her bottom lip, then said, "We talked about it."

"And he wasn't in favor of it?"

"No."

"Was . . . was Rod coming around?"

"No!" she said firmly. "He was not fighting with Rod over me."

"Okay," Clint said, "I'm just trying to get a clear picture."

"Maybe you better talk to Jeff, then," she said. "He can probably fill you in better than I can."

"I intend to talk to Jeff."

Now that that was settled there didn't seem to be anything else for them to talk about. They made some small talk while they finished the coffee, and then he got up to leave.

"Will you come and see me again while you're in town?" she asked, walking him to the door.

"Sure, I will," he said, not at all sure whether he was telling the truth or not.

NINE

Clint decided to talk to Jeff Banks right away rather than waiting until the next day. The place to find Banks, he was sure, was the mine. That made it necessary for him to walk the length of town, which, at this time in the life of Rock Springs, was not difficult. He then had to walk further to get to the office of the Rock Springs Mining Development Company, and then further still to get to the actual mines, some of which had been abandoned by now.

There was a foreman's shack at the mine, and Clint expected to find Jeff Banks there. He was right.

"Adams," Banks said, letting Clint into the shack, "sure, I remember you. In fact, you're one of my bosses, aren't you?"

"I don't think of it that way, Jeff," Clint said.

"Want a drink?" Banks asked. "I've got some whiskey here somewhere."

Banks had a head of prematurely white hair, which looked odd when you considered that he was still in his mid-thirties. He was a handsome man, though, and the white hair seemed to add to his appeal to women, if Clint remembered correctly.

"No, thanks," Clint said. "I'm fine."

"Well, then, what can I do for you?"

Banks folded his arms across his chest and waited. He

31

was a tall, broad-shouldered man who had once worked in the mines himself, and Clint thought that he must have been a hell of a productive miner.

"I'd like to talk about Sam Crider."

Banks's face fell.

"Goddamn it," he said, "but that's a shame. What a waste."

"Yes, it was," Clint said.

"Sam was a good man, Adams," Banks said, "ask anyone who worked here. He was damned good to the men who worked for him."

"Why are they ready to strike, then?"

"Well," Banks said, "if you ask me—and I guess you are—I'd say it was Craig's doing."

"Why's that?"

"The demands the men are making are not outlandish," Banks said, "but that Craig, he opposed giving in to any of them."

"Which side are you on in this dispute, Jeff?" Clint asked.

"Well," Banks said, scratching at his head, "I guess I'm in the middle, ain't I? I work for the company, like the other men, but the men also work for me."

"Whose side would you support if you were on the outside looking in?" Clint asked.

"If that was the case I wouldn't have all the facts, would I?" Banks asked.

"And do you now?"

"I doubt it," Banks said. "Craig plays his hand close to the vest. I pretty much knew what Sam was thinking, but I never know what's going on in Craig's head."

Clint thought that the fact that Banks referred to Crider by his first name and Craig by his last spoke volumes about how he felt about the two men.

"Who do you think would have reason to kill Sam Crider?"

Banks frowned.

"What are you talking about? They've got the guy who killed him in jail. That Chinaman, what's his name, Lee Too?"

"Lee To."

"Yeah, him."

"I was just wondering what your thoughts were, Jeff," Clint said. "If you thought there was anyone else who might have wanted him dead?"

"Why would you think about somebody else when his killer's in jail?"

Knowing now how Banks felt about Crider, Clint knew this wasn't going to be easy to explain.

"Let me talk here for a minute, Jeff," Clint said, "and then we can discuss what I say. Okay?"

"Sure," Banks said. "Go ahead."

Clint went through it slowly and, he hoped, logically, explaining his reasons for thinking that Lee To was innocent. True to his word, Banks listened until Clint was finished.

"So?" Clint asked. "What do you think?"

"I'm thinking that if you weren't one of my bosses I'd whip you to within an inch of your life."

"Now, Jeff—"

"Hell, I may do it, anyway."

"Jeff—"

"What's wrong with you?" Banks demanded. "I thought Sam Crider was your friend."

"He was—"

"Then how can you want his killer to go free? Answer me that."

"I'm sorry, Jeff," Clint said, "but I just don't think Lee To did it."

"When did you get to town?"

"Today," Clint said, "but—"

"Then how can you know anything?"

"When I heard about Sam I went to the jail to talk to the sheriff," Clint explained. "When I got there I talked to Lee To, as well."

"And he convinced you he didn't kill Sam?"

"Yes," Clint said, "he did."

Banks glared at Clint for a few moments, then walked to the door of the little shack and opened it.

"I think you better get out of here before I forget who you are."

"Jeff—"

"Just get out."

Clint walked to the door but stopped short of going through it.

"Can we talk again some other time?"

"Sure," Banks said, then added, "as long as it's about company business."

Clint stared at Banks for a few moments, then turned to leave.

"I'll tell you what I'll do," Banks said, before he could leave.

"What?"

"I'll give you some advice."

"Okay."

"All this stuff you told me? Don't tell it to any of the men who work here."

"Jeff, I don't think—"

"They were all loyal to Sam Crider," Banks went on, "and if they find out that you're in favor of letting his killer get away with it—well, I don't know what they'd do."

Clint waited a moment and when it was clear that Banks was finished he said, "I'll keep that in mind, Jeff. Thanks."

Clint stepped out of the shack then, and Banks closed the door with a resounding slam.

TEN

Clint decided he had asked enough questions for one day. He went to the saloon, which at this time of the evening was doing a brisk business. There were a couple of faro tables, and plenty of girls working the floor. He had been in Leadville recently, and this was not nearly as busy as that mining town, but the earmarks were all there. If Rock Springs kept growing, it would soon be another Leadville, Colorado.

He went to the bar, found a space, and ordered a beer.

"Did you get to see your friend?" the bartender asked as he served the beer.

"My friend?" Clint felt as if he had seen so many people that day.

"Mr. Craig, over at the mine?"

"Oh, Craig," Clint said. "Yeah, I saw him."

"How's he doin'?"

"He looked like he was doing pretty well to me," Clint said.

"It's too bad about his partner," the bartender said. "Too bad."

"You know," Clint said, "maybe you could help me with something."

"What's that you said?"

"Maybe you could help me—"

"Why don't you come down to the end of the bar?"

the man said. "There's room there and I'll be able to hear you better."

"All right," Clint said. He picked up his beer and followed the bartender to the other end of the bar. It seemed just as noisy to Clint, but the bartender was able to lean over a bit further when they talked.

"Now, what were you saying?"

"What's your name?"

"Oh," the bartender said, sticking out his hand, "the name's Benton. Most people just call me Ben."

"Ben, you hear a lot of things," Clint said. "Did you ever hear anybody complaining about Sam Crider?"

"Complainin'?"

"Yeah, you know," Clint said, "maybe somebody who wasn't happy with the way things were running at the mine?"

The bartender rubbed his jaw thoughtfully.

"Heard lots of people complainin' about the mine," he said. "You know, they're talkin' about goin' on strike."

"I heard that."

Now the bartender scratched his face, just below his left eye where there was a little scar.

"Never heard nobody complain about Mr. Crider directly," he said.

"I see."

"Heard them complain about Mr. Craig, though," he said.

"But Craig is still alive."

"Why are you askin' about somebody havin' somethin' against Mr. Crider?" the bartender asked. "Ain't they got the killer over at the jail?"

"Well, they've got somebody in jail," Clint said.

"That Chinaman, right?"

"Right."

"And didn't he kill 'im?"

"I don't know, Ben," Clint said. "I guess that's going to be for a court to decide, isn't it?"

"I guess," Ben said. "You just don't sound too sure, is all, Mr. Adams."

Clint didn't say anything to that.

"Hey, didn't you say you was gonna talk to the sheriff?"

"I did."

"And didn't he tell you that the Chinese done it?" Ben asked.

Clint didn't want to have this conversation again today. There were enough people mad at him.

"That's what he said, Ben," Clint said. "You know, I think I'll take a little walk around the bar."

"Yeah," Ben said, "you go ahead. I got the best girls in town workin' this place, don't let nobody tell you different."

"I'm sure you do," Clint said.

He took his beer and started walking around. As he did so he listened to the conversations going on, and the popular topic of discussion was the murder of Sam Crider. The consensus in town seemed to be that Lee To had done the killing, and nobody was really planning to look any further. He thought about Jeff Banks's advice earlier that evening. Asking more questions around town sure wasn't going to make him real popular.

Still, Crider was his friend, and if nobody else in town was going to try to find out who really killed him, then it was going to fall to him.

He had made a complete circuit of the room and was coming back to the bar when he noticed a new group of men standing there at the end, where he had been talking to Ben. He counted four, and they looked like miners, not ranch hands, or gunmen, or locals.

Miners who had worked for Sam Crider, and who were looking at him in none too friendly a fashion.

Clint was caught with an empty beer mug and no place to put it, unless he wanted to set it down on somebody else's table. He decided to just keep going to the bar, where he would set it down and then leave.

At least, that was his intention.

ELEVEN

Clint approached the bar and set the empty mug down on it.

"Another one?" Ben asked.

"I don't think so."

"Those boys are buyin'."

Clint frowned.

"Who?"

Ben indicated the four men at the end of the bar and said, "Those boys from the mine. They said they wanted to buy you a beer."

"Why?"

Ben shrugged.

"They didn't say that."

"Well," Clint said, "you tell them I said thanks, but some other time."

He turned to leave and heard somebody call out, "Hey, you."

He could have kept walking, but he knew "hey, you," was directed toward him. He turned and faced the four men, who had fanned out from the bar. The second one from the left spoke.

"You too good to have a drink bought for you by us?" he asked.

"Why do you want to buy me a drink?" Clint asked. "I don't know you, and you don't know me."

"But we got somethin' in common," the man said.

"What's that?"

"Sam Crider."

"What about him?"

"Well, the way I hear it, you were a friend of his."

"So?"

"So . . . *we* was friends of his, too."

"You look more like a bunch of men who worked for him," Clint said.

The man took offense.

"You sayin' you can't be friends with somebody you work for?"

"It isn't usually done."

"Well, we say we was friends of his," the man said. "You callin' us liars?"

Clint looked at each of the four men.

"Are you speaking for all these men?" he asked.

"That's right."

"Well," Clint said, "I'm not about to call the four of you liars."

"That's good," the man said, "that's real good."

"But I'm not about to have a drink with you, either."

That made the man bristle again.

"Why not?"

"Because the four of you are looking for trouble," Clint said. "I don't know if it's on your own, or if someone sent you, but you're looking for trouble, and I'm not about to oblige you."

"What if we made you oblige us?"

"You couldn't."

"Why not?"

"Because I have a gun, and you don't."

"You'd shoot an unarmed man?"

"No . . . but I'd shoot four unarmed men. See, I figure I'd be justified in shooting the four of you, rather than risk taking a beating from you."

The man hesitated, then asked, "You'd do that?"

"In a minute."

The spokesman exchanged a glance with his three friends, none of whom looked very sure of themselves at that moment.

"I think you'd better go back to whoever sent you and find out who you're dealing with, boys," Clint said. "You'll find out that this could have cost you your jobs."

"Huh?"

"See?" Clint said. "Go ask some questions, and think next time before you agree to do something."

He turned and left the four of them standing there looking and feeling puzzled.

The spokesman looked at the bartender and asked, "Would he have done it?"

"That man?" the bartender said. "Yeah, he would have."

TWELVE

Clint went to his hotel room and pulled off his boots. He sat on the edge of the bed and rubbed his feet. How did he get himself into these situations? All he'd wanted to do was check on his investment and say hello to a couple of friends. Now one was dead and he wasn't sure he was even on speaking terms with the other one anymore.

And what about the men in the saloon? Who had sent them after him, without telling them who he was? Rod Craig? Or Jeff Banks?

He removed his gun belt, hung it on the bedpost, took off his trousers, opened his shirt, and went to the pitcher and basin on the dresser. He washed up and decided to go to bed early. He'd ridden most of the day and had had no rest since he'd arrived in town. He'd talked to a lot of people and gotten very little satisfaction. He didn't want to think about Sam Crider's death anymore until the morning. Over breakfast he'd decide what his next move should be.

"You didn't tell us he was Clint Adams," one of the four men said. He had been the spokesman in the bar, and so was the more upset of the four. After all, *he* had threatened the Gunsmith.

"We coulda got killed!" one of the other men said.

43

"How did you find out?"

"We was told, that's how," the third man said.

The fourth man remained silent. He hadn't said a word since they'd found out that the man they were threatening was Clint Adams, the Gunsmith.

"What was you tryin' to do?" the first man asked. "Get us killed?"

The four of them stared at the other man, waiting for an answer.

"He wouldn't have killed you," the man finally said.

"Oh no?"

"You were unarmed."

"He said he'd rather kill us than take a beatin'," the first man said.

"And you believed him?"

"Damn right, we did."

"We all did," the second man said.

The names of the four men were of no consequence to the fifth. He had paid them to start a fight with a man and teach him a lesson, and it hadn't worked. He had no use for them any longer.

"Get out," he said, "the four of you."

"What about the rest of our money?" the first man asked.

"You're lucky I don't make you give back what I already gave you," the fifth man said. "Now get out!"

Grudgingly, the four men shuffled out the door, letting it close behind them.

So his plan had backfired. It had only been one plan. He had others. For instance, he was sure he could still incite a mob of miners to storm the jail, pull that Chinaman out, and hang him. It just needed the right timing.

Killing Sam Crider had simply been the first step, and he wasn't about to let anyone—not even Clint Adams—get in the way of the steps that were still to come.

THIRTEEN

Clint woke early the next morning, feeling refreshed. His first night in a real bed, after sleeping on the trail, often left him feeling this way. It was one of the reasons he still hadn't settled down in one place. He didn't want to start taking the night's sleep in a real bed for granted.

He washed up, dressed, strapped on his gun, and went downstairs for breakfast.

He ate his food slowly, idly watching the other diners in the hotel dining room, and thinking about Sam Crider. He still had a connection to Rock Springs, and to Rod Craig, through his investment in the mining company. He could have forgotten about the death of Sam Crider, allowed Craig to buy him out and be done with the whole thing—but he couldn't do that. Not without knowing who had killed Crider, and why. Losing friends was just not something he was good at, and it was not something that he could walk away from. If there were people in town who didn't like him asking questions, then that was just too bad, because the questions were going to get asked.

He thought about the four miners in the saloon last night. He still figured there was only one of two men who could have sent them. Either Rod Craig or Jeff Banks. Or, taking the scenario a little further, Craig

45

could have told Banks to pick out four men for the job and then send them—except for one thing. Banks struck Clint as the kind of man who would have chosen his men better.

He drank his second pot of coffee while considering his options. There didn't seem to be any new people to talk to. He figured he'd just have to go back to Virginia, and Craig, and Banks, and even the sheriff, and talk to them all again. Maybe he needed to talk to the men in the mines, except they were getting ready to go on strike. He'd been able to back four men down last night, but if he went to the mines and started asking questions, he'd be facing a lot more than four men.

It was pretty clear that he needed an ally, but who could that be? Among the three people who seemed the most likely—Virginia, Craig, and Banks—Virginia was the one who came to mind. She was the one he had once had a very close—physically close—relationship with. Maybe because of that she would be willing to help him—all he'd have to do is convince her. Convince her that Lee To wasn't the killer, and convince her that she should help him find out who the real killer was.

After all, she had been Sam Crider's woman, so how hard could that be?

FOURTEEN

Virginia owned and ran a dress shop in town. Clint knew that from a letter he'd received from Crider earlier that year. When Clint had last been in Rock Springs there had been no dress shop.

To get to the shop from his hotel he had to pass the jail. As he did so he saw three people going into the jail, two men and a woman. They were all Chinese. Curiosity got the better of him, and he stopped at the door. He heard agitated voices from inside and decided to go in.

As he entered he saw the sheriff standing behind his desk, and he was arguing with the three Chinese—only it sounded like they were speaking their own language.

"Look," Sheriff Reasoner said, "you're gonna have to talk English if you want me to understand you."

The woman seemed to translate what he'd said to the two men, who fell silent.

"My father and uncle do not speak English," she said. "I will speak for them."

"That's fine, ma'am," Reasoner said, and then noticed Clint standing inside the door. He raised a hand to him, letting him know he'd be with him in a minute.

The three Chinese also turned to look at Clint. The two men frowned at him, but it was the woman's face he noticed the most. He'd seen a lot of Oriental women over the years, especially in both San Francisco's and

47

New York's Chinatowns, but hers was the loveliest Oriental face he'd ever seen. Her eyes were somewhat larger than most Chinese he had seen, and her lips were full and wider.

"Now what's all the fuss about, ma'am?" Reasoner asked the woman.

She, her father, and her uncle turned their attention back to the lawman.

"They want to know when you are going to let Lee To out of jail," she said.

"I can't do that, ma'am," he said. He looked at the men and repeated himself. "I can't do that." Then he looked at the woman again, realizing the men couldn't understand him. "Tell them I can only let him out when a judge tells me to let him go."

She turned and translated and both men began chattering at her at one time.

"They want to know when that will be."

"I can't say, ma'am," Reasoner said. "I don't know when the judge is coming to town."

She translated this, as well.

"Will we be permitted to bring him food?"

"Well, I feed my prisoners, ma'am, I don't see why—" He didn't get a chance to finish, as she cut him off.

"We would like to cook for him."

"Ma'am, that don't seem—"

"Why can't they cook for him, Sheriff?" Clint asked. "I mean, I don't mean to butt in, but where's the harm?"

Reasoner frowned at the interruption, but then said, "Oh, all right, I guess there's no real harm in it, but you can only bring it to him when I'm here."

"We will do that," she said.

"Is there anything else?" the lawman asked her.

She exchanged some words with her uncle and father,

then looked at him and said, "No, nothing else. We will leave now."

They turned and walked to the door. The two men ignored Clint as they shuffled by, but the young woman—she couldn't have been more than twenty—boldly met his eyes before walking past him.

"What brings you here, Adams?" Reasoner asked, sitting down.

"You know," Clint said, "I got so involved in your conversation with them, I forgot. I'll come back when I remember."

"Fine," Reasoner said with a wave.

Clint backed out of the jail and closed the door behind him. He looked for the three Chinese, and when he spotted them he hurried to catch up.

FIFTEEN

"Excuse me?" he called out.

Only the woman turned because she was the only one who understood. The men kept going.

"Yes?" she asked. "You wish to speak to me?"

"Yes, I do."

"I must get back to our camp," she said. "You may walk with me, if you like."

"Thank you," he said. "I will."

They started walking and she maintained a steady pace without hurrying to catch up to the other two.

"I was just wondering . . . is Lee To your husband?" he asked.

She seemed to find that funny.

"No, he is not."

"Brother, then? Cousin?"

"We are not related."

"Then he isn't related to either of those gentlemen who were with you?"

"No," she said. "They are my father and my uncle, and they are not related to him."

"Is he your boyfriend, then?"

"Boyfriend?"

"Do you love him?"

"Oh, no," she said, "it is nothing like that. He is part of our group, that is all."

51

"Where did you come here from?"

"San Francisco."

"And he came with you?"

"Oh, no," she said, "we were here already when Lee came along. He wandered into our camp and we invited him to stay. That is all."

"I see. How many of you are there in the camp?"

She shrugged and said, "Forty or fifty—but there are other camps. We are here to work in the mines."

"If there is a strike, you mean?"

"Well, some of us already work in the mines, but if there is a strike we will continue."

"Don't you consider that dangerous?"

She shrugged as they cleared the outskirts of town and kept walking.

"We must eat," she said simply.

"Do you believe that Lee To killed Mr. Crider?" he asked.

"No," she said, shaking her head, "we know he did not do that."

"How do you know?"

"He told us."

"And you believe him?"

"Why should we not?"

"Does everyone in camp believe him?"

"Of course," she said. "Lee To would have no reason to kill Mr. Crider."

"I thought Crider didn't want your people working the mines during a strike?"

"That may be so," she said, "but that is not a reason to kill him."

When they reached the camp Clint was the center of attention.

"Do many of your people here speak English?" he asked the girl.

"Some do, some don't," she said. "Why?"

"I'd like to ask some questions," he said.

"About what?"

"About that night," he said, "the night of the killing."

"Why?"

He shrugged. "Maybe somebody saw something."

She turned to face him then.

"You don't believe Lee To kill Mr. Crider?"

"No, I don't."

"Why do you care?"

"Because Sam Crider was my friend," he said. "I want to know who really killed him."

She stared at him for a few moments, then asked, "What is your name?"

"Clint Adams."

She nodded. "I have heard of you."

They stood in silence for a moment, and then she said, "I will help you. I will translate for the ones who do not speak English."

"Thank you," he said. "What is your name?"

"Jean," she said, then added, "that is my American name. Jean."

"Well, Jean," he said, "why don't we get started? There are a lot of people here to talk to."

"Will you want to talk to the others? In the other camps?"

"Yes."

"Then you are right," she said. "We should get started."

They managed to get through the people in Jean's camp and then it got dark.

"I'll have to talk to the others tomorrow," he said. "I should be getting back to town."

"You may eat with us, if you like," she said. "After,

I can walk back to town with you and bring Lee To
some food.''

"All right," he said. "Thank you."

"Thank you," she said. "I will feel better walking to
town in the dark with you."

"Then we're helping each other," he said, "aren't
we?"

She smiled and said, "Yes."

SIXTEEN

Clint ate with Jean and her people but did not feel particularly welcome. She was really the only one who spoke to him. From across the fire her uncle and father regarded him suspiciously.

"What do they think I'm going to do?" he asked her.

"They just distrust you," she said. "They distrust all *lo fan*."

Clint had heard the term *"lo fan"* before. It was the way the Chinese referred to white people.

Clint wasn't sure what he was eating. Some kind of meat, certainly, and vegetables, but he wasn't sure he really wanted to know what the meat was. He'd eaten snake and, while among Indians, had even eaten dog. He didn't need to know what this was.

When they were finished Jean prepared a meal for Lee To, and then she and Clint walked back to town with it. It was dark, but not late. As they reentered town they could hear noise coming from the saloon. Clint remembered what the sheriff had said about only bringing Lee To food while he was there, and he hoped they would not find the sheriff's office empty and locked.

They were in luck and Reasoner told them so.

"I was just gonna go and get myself some dinner."

"Why don't you?" Clint asked. "We'll be here."

Reasoner thought about that, then nodded. He stood up, then stopped and looked at Clint.

"If he gets away—"

"I'm not going to let him out," Clint said. "That would make him a wanted man. Besides, he doesn't strike me as the type to run."

"I'll take you at your word, Adams," Reasoner said. "I should be gone an hour."

"Fine."

Reasoner left and Clint took Jean into the back so she could give Lee To his food.

"If you wait while he eats it," Clint said, "and until the sheriff comes back, I'll walk you back to camp."

"I will wait," she said.

Lee To began eating, and while he was doing so he and Jean had a conversation in Chinese. At least part of the time Clint felt they were talking about him. He heard the term "*lo fan*" more than once, but they didn't necessarily have to be talking about him each time it was said.

"You have been asking questions?" Lee To asked him.

"Yes."

"And have you found out anything?"

"Only that everyone thinks you're guilty."

"But I am not."

"I know that."

"Have you told them?"

"Yes," Clint said, "but there's no reason for them to believe me."

"Or me," Lee To said.

"Yes."

"You are worried?" Jean asked.

Lee To put the remainder of his dinner down on the floor of the cell.

"I am starting to worry, yes," he said. "What if a judge does not believe me either?"

"But he must," Jean said. "You did not do it."

"This man seems to be the only one, other than our own people, who believes that."

"Well, then, he will prove it," Jean said, looking at Clint.

"I'll try," he said.

"Why?" Lee asked. "Why would you do that for me?"

"I'm doing it for me," Clint said. "I want to know who really killed my friend."

"And when you find out," Lee said, "I will go free."

"Yes."

Lee pushed his food tray over to the door where Jean could slide it through the slot designed for that purpose.

"Then I will wait," Lee To said, and it sounded odd to Clint that the man made it sound as if he had a choice in the matter.

SEVENTEEN

Clint and Jean left the jail after Sheriff Reasoner returned. They were walking toward the edge of town when three men stepped from the shadows. These were not miners, but men armed with guns, who looked as if they knew how to use them.

"Hey, Chinee gal," one of them said. "You wanna have a party with us?"

"I do not have time," Jean said, "and if I did, I would not spend it with you."

"Hey, Roy," one of the other men said, "that sounded like an insult to me. Did it sound like an insult to you, Henry?"

"It sounded like an insult to me," the third man said. "How about you, Roy?"

"It sounded right unfriendly to me," the man named Roy said. "Mister," he said to Clint, "you think you'd be willin' to share your woman with us?"

"No," Clint said.

Jean was in front of Clint and now she backed up until she was pressed against him. Clint took her by the shoulders and moved her so that she was standing behind him.

"Why don't you boys go on over to the saloon," he suggested. "There are plenty of women over there who'd be pleased to party with you."

"Yeah, but they ain't Chinee," Roy said. "See, to-night we got a hankerin' to party with a Chinee gal. Now, that's a Chinee gal you got there, and she's a right pretty one. And you know what? We pick her."

"Well," Clint said, "she doesn't pick you. I'd advise you boys to move aside and let us pass."

At the moment Clint couldn't decide if this was an-other case of these boys being sent to pick a fight, or if this had nothing to do with Sam Crider's death. Maybe these were just some drunk boys out looking for a good time, and they were looking in the wrong direction.

"Mister," Roy said, "they's three of us an' only one of you. What you wanna go and be unfriendly for?"

"There may be three of you," Clint said, "but it seems to me like you boys are a mite drunk, and I'm not. Now, in your condition you're probably none of you going to hit me with your first shot."

"Shot?" Roy said, looking at his friends. "Who's talkin' about shootin'?" He looked at his two friends again. "You boys talkin' about shootin' somebody?"

"Not me, Roy," Henry said.

"Me either," said the other man, whose name Clint had not yet heard.

"See?" Roy said, a congenial look on his face, "no-body's talkin' about shooting." The congeniality dropped from his face abruptly and he added, "But if that's how you want it, friend."

"Over a girl?" Clint asked. "Is that what you want to die over?"

"Over what we want," Roy said. "See, we generally get what we want."

"Let me ask you something before the shooting starts," Clint said.

"What?"

"Were you hired to do this," Clint asked, "or is it your own stupid idea?"

Roy went for his gun, bringing the whole conversation to a halt in a hail of gunfire. When it was over the three men were lying in the street and Clint was untouched. So was the girl behind him.

So were the guns of the three men, which were still snugly in their holsters.

"What the hell—" Sheriff Reasoner shouted, coming out of his office with his gun in his hand.

Clint turned and saw the sheriff coming. He put his gun hand up over his head.

"The shooting's over, Sheriff," Clint said, waving his gun.

Other people were coming out onto the street from some of the surrounding buildings, including a big crowd from the saloon. Clint looked around, trying to find a familiar face, but he saw none. If someone he knew had hired these three to shoot it out with him, that person had apparently not stayed around to watch it.

"What the hell happened here?" Reasoner demanded, looking down at the three dead men.

"They started it," Jean said, still standing behind Clint.

"That true, Adams?" Reasoner asked.

"That's the way it was," Clint said. "Do you mind if I reload my gun and put it away while we talk?"

Reasoner looked around, then holstered his gun while Clint ejected his spent shells, replaced them, and holstered his own.

"Let me take a look at these three first," he said, "and then we'll go into my office and talk about it."

Clint noticed some Chinese faces in the crowd all of a sudden.

"Do you see anyone you know?" he asked Jean.

"Yes," she said, "someone from my camp."

"You go with them, then," Clint said, "let them walk you home."

"But—"

"It's all right," he said, "you go on."

Hesitantly, she stepped out from behind him and went to join the men from her camp.

"Hey, where is she going?" Reasoner demanded.

"She's going back to her camp."

"She's a witness."

"She told you what she saw," Clint said. "Let her go home."

"But—"

"Do you know those three?"

"No," Reasoner said, still not happy. "Never saw them before."

"Then they just got to town today?" Clint asked.

"I don't know," Reasoner said. "Hey, Charlie, Ed, get some men and move these fellas off the street, huh?"

"Take them to the undertaker's, Sheriff?" Charlie asked.

"I can't think of anyplace else they'd rather be right now," Reasoner said. "Also, I want all you people who are out here on the street to make yourselves useful. Take a look at these men and tell me if you've seen them before. Maybe you know 'em, maybe they were just in your store. Let me know."

He turned to Clint and said, "Let's go into my office and you can tell me what happened."

They turned and walked toward the jail together.

"You handled that real well."

"Yeah, well," Reasoner said, rubbing the back of his head, "I ain't Wyatt Earp, but I'm learning the job."

EIGHTEEN

Inside the office Clint told the sheriff what had happened in the street.

"So this was over the girl?"

"That's the way it looks."

"And you didn't know them?"

"No."

"And did they know who you are?"

"They didn't seem to."

"Well, wherever they are now, they know."

"I suppose so."

The office door opened and the man the sheriff had called Charlie came in.

"They're at the undertaker's, Sheriff."

"Good, thanks, Charlie. Anybody out there recognize them?"

"There's a coupla folks out here waiting to talk to you."

"Send them in, will you?"

"Sure thing."

Charlie left and two men stepped in. Neither of them was armed, and they were likely town merchants. Clint thought he recognized one of them. A third came in behind them, and Clint recognized the bartender from the saloon, Ben, who spoke first.

"Sheriff, I got to get back to work."

"What do you know, Ben?"

"Not much," he said. "I just seen them in the saloon is all."

"When?"

"Earlier in the day, and then again tonight."

"They seem like trouble to you?"

"No more than anybody else."

"Were they in there when I was?" Clint asked.

"Can't say for sure."

"Were they with any of your girls?"

"Can't say that either."

"Ask 'em, will you, Ben?" the sheriff said. "And let me know."

"Sure thing, Sheriff. Can I go?"

"Yeah, go ahead."

Ben left, then Reasoner looked at the other two men.

"What have you two got to say?"

One of the men ran a small café at the end of town and he said he thought one of the dead men had eaten there.

"Did he talk much?"

"Naw," the man said. "He ate alone."

"Ever see him before today?"

"No."

The other man owned the livery, and he had the most useful information to give. He was the one Clint had thought he recognized.

"They rode into town this afternoon and left their horses with me."

"When was that exactly, Lem?"

"Can't say for sure. Just after noon, I guess."

"Did they see my horse?" Clint asked.

"Don't know. They didn't mention him."

Clint looked at Reasoner.

"So they just got to town today and picked a fight with you tonight," Reasoner said.

"That's the way it sounds."

"You fellas can go," Reasoner said.

Both men nodded and left.

"What do you think about this, Adams? If they didn't recognize you, were they really after the girl?"

"I don't know, Sheriff," Clint said. "I've been asking questions around town, you know, about Sam Crider's death. Some miners tried to pick a fight with me earlier, but I talked them out of it."

"Too bad you couldn't have talked these fellas out of it, as well."

"I agree with you there," Clint said, "believe me."

Reasoner worried the back of his neck again.

"Can't see as I've got any reason to hold you," he said.

"I wasn't looking for this, Sheriff."

"I didn't think you were," Reasoner said. "Go ahead, then, and try not to shoot anyone else."

"I'll give it my best shot . . . no joke intended, Sheriff."

"Go on," Reasoner said, waving a weary hand, "get out of here."

After the shooting one man stood behind some of the others in the crowd, so he couldn't be readily seen. He saw the three men on the ground, and Clint Adams standing without a scratch. He'd been watching, too, from a darkened doorway, and had been amazed at the speed with which the Gunsmith had produced his gun. He'd heard stories about the man, legends even, but he'd never seen anything so fast in his life.

Even before Clint and the sheriff left the street this man had turned and pushed his way out of the crowd. He had a report to make, and he figured he'd better get out while there was still a crowd to hide in. Now that he'd seen the Gunsmith in action he was going to make his report, collect his money, and then get out of town. He didn't want any part of a man who could handle his gun like that.

NINETEEN

Clint left the sheriff's office and stood just outside. There were still some men milling about, talking about the shooting, but for the most part the crowd had cleared out. He stepped into the street and started for the hotel, and the remaining men gave him a wide berth.

Walking to the hotel he went over the incident again in his mind. He was fairly certain that the men hadn't known who he was. Also, they seemed drunk, but he hadn't been close enough to actually smell whiskey on them. It could have been an act.

And had they really wanted the girl? Had they died—gotten themselves killed—simply because they wanted a young Chinese girl? With all the girls who were available at the saloon?

What a waste. Clint was suddenly angry with the men for forcing his hand and making him kill them. He hoped they had been hired to brace him, because then at least he could think that he had killed them while they were doing a job. To have killed them in a squabble over a woman—any woman—left a bad taste in his mouth. He'd killed men before in the defense of a woman, but never in a fight over a woman.

More and more it seemed as if Jean had been just a useful excuse to start a fight. If that was the case, then

67

they'd been sent, or hired, probably by the same person who had sent the miners after him.

At least, he hoped it was the same person. If it wasn't, then there were two people who were out to get him.

As he reached the hotel he remembered that he'd been on his way to talk with Virginia again when he'd been waylaid by seeing Jean and her uncle and father go into the sheriff's office. He was going to have to go talk to her first thing tomorrow.

He walked into the lobby and was surprised to see Virginia sitting there, her hands primly in her lap, although there was nothing else prim about her. She was wearing a cotton dress that clung to her, and her hair was worn down—it, and her skin, smelling from a fresh bath.

"Virginia."

She looked up at him, then stood up and approached him, one hand out, then withdrawn.

"I thought we should talk again," she said. "I was going to wait until tomorrow, but then I heard about the shooting. Are you all right?"

"I'm fine," Clint said, "but there are three men over at the undertaker's, and I have no idea who they were."

"But . . . this has happened to you before, men wanting to . . . to try you?"

"These men didn't seem to know who I am," Clint said. "I think they were sent."

"By who?"

"I don't know."

"Who would want you dead?"

"Whoever killed Sam Crider, maybe," Clint said. "I've been asking a lot of questions."

"But . . . but if that's why they tried to kill you," she said, "then you must be right. The Chinaman didn't kill Sam."

"I've thought I was right from the beginning, Virginia," he said. "I didn't need this to convince me."

"We have to talk, then," she said. "Can we . . . go up to your room?"

"Sure," he said. "Come on."

They walked past the desk, ignoring the look from the desk clerk, and went up to his room. Outside his room he stopped her.

"What is it?"

"Just let me check the room first," he said, drawing his gun.

She stood back while he unlocked the door, then flung it open and dashed inside, going down to one knee.

"It's all right," he said after a moment. "Wait, I'll turn up the light."

He turned the flame up on the lamp on the wall and then let her enter.

"You must get tired of having to enter hotel rooms like that."

"It's not always that bad," he said, "but after what's happened today . . . Sit down, Virginia."

She sat on the bed. He remained standing for the moment. He walked to the window and looked outside, satisfying himself that there was no access to the window. Only then did he undo his gun belt and hang it on the bedpost.

"I was on my way to see you today," he said, "but I got involved with something else."

"Why were you coming to see me?"

"I thought we should talk again, too."

"About what?"

"About Sam."

"That's what I wanted to talk to you about."

There was one chair in the room. He turned it around and straddled it, resting his arms on the back.

"What's on your mind, Virginia?"

"Sam."

"What about him?"

"The past few weeks he'd been real nervous."

"Did he say why?"

"I asked him a few times, but he didn't want to talk about it."

"What did you think it was?"

"Business."

"How were he and Rod getting along?"

"Not well. They were fighting . . . not over me, but over the business, the miners, the . . . the strike."

"Did he give you any specifics?"

"No, but it was affecting . . . us."

"How?"

"We didn't talk, we didn't do much of anything except . . . except go to bed, and even that had become . . . unsatisfying."

She fell silent and he decided to wait for her to continue.

"I think we were finished, Clint," she said. "I think it was just a matter of . . . days."

"I'm sorry."

"Don't be," she said. "It was never right between us anyway."

"Virginia . . ."

"You know the reason," she said, looking at him.

"I don't think—"

"It was you," she said. "He was just a replacement for you."

"Now, Virginia—"

"You were right about one thing," she said.

"What was that?"

"You said you knew I'd end up with Rod or Sam, you just didn't know which one. To me it was about the same, but I always thought that you were better friends with Sam."

"You're right," he said, "I was."

"Well, that's why I picked Sam," she said. "That's the only reason."

"But you were together six months . . ."

"He tried," she said, "he tried real hard for a while to make me happy. I think he . . . he knew that he was a substitute for you."

Clint remembered some of Sam Crider's letters. He hadn't mentioned much in them about Virginia, but what man would, if he thought he was writing to the man he was a poor substitute for.

"Virginia," he said, "you never told him that, did you?"

"No," she said, "not even when we argued. I never would have . . . hurt him that way."

Clint was relieved at that.

"Virginia, see if there's more you can tell me about the last few days before he died."

"Well, he was nervous about the strike," she said. "He was talking with the miners, trying to get them to listen to reason. And he was talking to Rod, trying the same thing. It was like he was stuck in the middle and just couldn't get them together."

"Rod wouldn't budge, huh?"

She shook her head.

"Not at all."

Clint rubbed his jaw thoughtfully.

"I guess I'm going to have to talk to the miners."

"They'll kill you."

"Maybe not," Clint said. "Maybe I can make them listen to reason, see that it's better to make sure we know who really killed Sam."

"Will they listen to you?"

"I'll have to hope they will."

There was an awkward silence then, Virginia sitting with her hands in her lap, Clint standing, and then she stood up and moved closer to him.

"Virginia—"

"I told you Sam and I were through, Clint," she said, "that he was a substitute for you."

"Virginia . . ."

"It was never the way it was with you," she said, putting her arms around his neck, "never."

Before he could protest again she pulled his head down to kiss him, and then he was lost in her lips.

TWENTY

They undressed each other quickly and tumbled onto the bed. Her body was as he remembered it, full and responsive. She was so eager that he couldn't imagine that sex between her and Sam had been unsatisfying.

He kissed her breasts, lingering over the nipples, and she purred and held his head in her hands. Then he moved down over her belly to her crotch, where she was wet and fragrant. He put his tongue to work, and again she grabbed his head, but she didn't purr this time, she growled.

"Oh, God, I've missed that," she said as his tongue moved over her. "Ooh, yes, right . . . there!"

He slid his hands beneath her to cup her buttocks and lift her off the bed so he could have better access to lick her more fully. He worked his tongue up and down, in and out, then found her clit and flicked it, circled it, sucked it until she was bucking and crying out and pulling his hair. . . .

"I never let myself think about how much I missed you," she said, lying on his shoulder with his arm around her. "Did you miss me?"

"Virginia—"

"No, don't answer that," she said. "If the answer's no, I don't want to—"

73

"Yes," he said, "I missed you."

She snuggled up against him and said, "Good."

They lay there quietly for a while, and she spoke just when he was beginning to think she'd fallen asleep.

"Do you feel bad?"

"About what?"

"About . . . this, about Sam."

"I feel bad about Sam being dead."

"But not about being here with me . . . like this?"

"No," he said, "not at all."

"Because you shouldn't, you know," she said. "You were first, after all—"

"Virginia?"

"What?"

"Go to sleep."

She snuggled in again and said, "Gladly."

Clint woke the next morning and for a moment he didn't know who he was with. Her back was to him, and the sheet had slid off. Her hair was fanned out, her skin was pale, and he admired the way the line of her spine led into the cleft between her butt cheeks . . . and he remembered.

He reached out and ran his hand over her hip, and her thighs, and then her butt, and still she slept. He didn't have the heart to wake her, even though he had an erection. He rolled onto his back and stared at the ceiling, willing it away. Finally, he was able to sit up and swing his feet to the floor.

He decided to dress quietly and leave, if he could, without waking her. He slipped out the door and stopped in the hall, wondering if he should have left her a note, then decided not to chance going back in. Instead, he went downstairs to the dining room to have breakfast.

He was the center of attention as soon as he entered the dining room. Obviously everyone had heard about the shooting. As he sat the waiter came over and he ordered coffee.

"Do you have a local newspaper?" he asked.

"Sure do," the waiter said, "but it's only a few pages. It's gonna get bigger, though."

"Do you have one I can read? Is it out yet?"

"Special morning edition came out just a little while ago," the waiter said. "I'll bring you one."

"Thanks."

True to his word, the waiter returned with coffee and the newspaper. Clint waited until he went away then looked at the front page. Sure enough, he was the head-line of the *Rock Springs Gazette*. GUNSMITH KILLS THREE IN LATE NIGHT SHOOT-OUT.

The story went on to say that he had killed three men in a fight over a Chinese girl from one of the camps. It also said that the sheriff considered the shoot-out a fair fight. "How can you jail one man for killing three?" the sheriff was quoted as saying. "He was outnumbered, and survived. You can't arrest a man for that."

"I see you're reading it."

It was a man's voice, and Clint looked up to see a man in his early thirties standing by his table.

"Reading what?"

"My story."

Clint looked at the name on the newspaper.

"You're John Standiford?"

"That's me. Editor, staff, and sweeper."

Clint folded the four-page newspaper and set it aside. At that moment the waiter came with his breakfast.

"Do you mind if I sit down, Mr. Adams?" Standiford asked.

"I'm having my breakfast."

"Well, perhaps we could do an interview after you've finished?"

"I don't think so."

"But . . . I'd like to hear your side."

"I don't do interviews."

"But, Mr. Adams, the people—"

Clint looked directly into the man's eyes and said, "You're interfering with my breakfast, Mr. Standiford."

"I—I'm—uh, sorry—" Standiford stammered and backed away from the table.

Clint called the waiter over.

"Yes, sir?"

"You can have your newspaper back."

"Yes, sir."

Clint tried to enjoy his breakfast, but the combination of the newspaper and its editor/staff/sweeper had already ruined it.

TWENTY-ONE

After breakfast Clint thought about going back upstairs and crawling back into bed with Virginia. It was a good idea, if he had had nothing else to do, but that wasn't the case. He had to find out who had killed Sam Crider.

When he came to Rock Springs, the last thing he'd expected he'd be doing was playing detective. It was a role he had been thrust into before, but he still did not consider himself one. Not the way Talbot Roper or some of Allan Pinkerton's people were.

He wanted to talk to the miners, but before he did that he wanted to talk to Rod Craig. He walked to the Rock Springs Mining Development Company and entered the office. Craig was sitting behind his desk, studying some charts. He looked up when Clint entered.

"Heard you had some trouble last night," he said.

"Who told you?"

Craig held up the local newspaper, then dropped it onto his desk.

"This the way it was?" he asked.

"There was a Chinese girl with me," Clint said, "but that's not the way it was. In fact, I think those three men were sent after me."

"By who?"

"That's what I want to find out," Clint said. "In fact,

three of your men tried to pick a fight with me, too, but they weren't armed."

"Three of my men?"

Clint nodded.

"Who the hell—hey, you don't think I sent them, do you?"

"I don't know who sent them, Rod."

"Well, it wasn't me."

"Okay," Clint said, "so how about your foreman, Jeff Banks? Would he do it?"

"Banks? Why?"

"To keep me from asking questions."

"Again, why?"

"I can think of two possible reasons," Clint said. "One, to keep me from proving that Lee To didn't kill Sam, and two, to keep me from proving Lee To didn't kill Sam."

Craig looked puzzled.

"That's the same thing."

"Not really," Clint said. "See, there are those who think Lee To's guilty, and they feel that my efforts to get him off are disrespectful to Sam's memory. Then there are those who know Lee To isn't guilty, and they're afraid I'll find out who is."

"Now, which one of those categories do you think I fall into?"

"I don't know, Rod," Clint said. "Maybe I'd just better ask some more questions."

Craig dropped his pencil on top of the chart and sat back in his chair.

"I don't know why I should answer them, but go ahead. Ask."

"I understand you and Sam were really split on the question of the strike."

"Neither of us wanted it," Craig said.

"But he was willing to bend, and you weren't."

"I wasn't willing to give into unreasonable demands, if that's what you mean."

"And then there was the question of the Chinese. Sam didn't want to use them, right?"

"Right," Craig said, "and if the men go on strike and we don't use them, we go out of business."

"And if the men go on strike and you do use them," Clint said, "you chance a riot."

"A riot may not happen," Craig said, "but we definitely would go out of business. I didn't see how we could take the chance."

"You said Sam was the one negotiating with the men."

"That's right."

"Who's doing it now?"

"I guess I will be."

"I have an idea."

"What?"

"Why don't you let me do it?"

"You? Why you? What do you know about strike negotiating?"

"Maybe nothing," Clint said, "but you're not good with people, are you, Rod?"

"No, I'm not," Craig said, "I'm good with charts."

"I need to talk to the men," Clint said, "and Banks warned me off."

"Why?"

"He said they were loyal to Sam and they wouldn't take kindly to me trying to get his killer off."

"He's probably right."

"But if I went to the men as a partner, and to negotiate the strike, they'd talk to me more readily, wouldn't they? And they wouldn't risk their jobs by trying to brace me."

"I guess you're right."

"So all we have to do is have Jeff introduce me around, and I'll take it from there."

Craig sat forward and picked up his pencil again.

"Unless you don't want me asking questions about Sam's death."

"Hell, no, ask all you want," Craig said. "It sounds like a good idea to me. I'll set it up with Jeff. When do you want to do it?"

"As soon as possible."

"Come by this afternoon, about one. I'll have Jeff briefed by then."

"Do me another favor."

"What's that?"

"Find out if he sent those men after me."

"What will you do to him?"

"You don't even have to tell me," Clint said. "Just make sure none of the miners come after me again."

Craig nodded and said, "I can do that—and if I find out he sent them I'll tear a couple layers off his hide."

"Don't fire him."

"Jesus, no, I wouldn't do that," Craig said. "With Sam gone I need Jeff more than ever."

"All right, then," Clint said. "I'll be back around one."

"We'll be ready."

Clint left Craig, still not sure of the man. Nothing had been said during the conversation that would clear him or incriminate him in Sam's death—or in sending those men after Clint. Still, one thing had been accomplished. Clint would now be able to talk to all of the men in an "official" capacity, and since they "worked" for him, they'd have to answer him.

TWENTY-TWO

The man stared at Rod Craig, who was seated behind his desk, as he had been when Clint Adams was there.

"Why did you agree to this?" he demanded.

"Because if I didn't," Craig said, "he would have been suspicious. Besides, he is an investor."

"Buy him out then."

"I don't have the money to do that," Craig said, "do you?"

The man didn't answer.

"What am I supposed to do now?" he asked instead.

"Do what you're paid to do, and do it yourself," Craig said. "Stop sending miners and drunks—"

"Okay," the man said, "don't fly off the handle. What the hell was Adams doin' with that Chinese gal last night, anyway?"

"The information I got was that he was in the jail with her, bringing that Chinaman some food."

"What's he gettin' involved with them for?"

"I don't know," Craig said, "but they can't tell him anything, so it doesn't do any harm."

"It's gonna look like he's on their side," the man said. "Your miners aren't gonna take kindly to that."

"My miners are going to find out today that Clint Adams is one of their bosses."

"That means they'll talk to him."

"Most of them will," Craig said, "and most of them can't hurt us."

"What about the ones who can?"

Craig thought about that for a moment.

"Maybe they should have some kind of accident."

"What kind of accident?"

"A mining accident," Craig said patiently. "What other kind of accident would you have in a mine?"

TWENTY-THREE

Clint stopped by Virginia's shop to kill some time until one.

"Why'd you sneak out this morning?" she asked, after her only customer left.

"I didn't have the heart to wake you," he said. "You were sleeping so soundly."

"And you're the reason why," she said. "My body hasn't been this relaxed since . . . well, in six months. You were wonderful! Even better than I remem—"

"You're going to give me a swelled head," he said.

She smiled and said, "That's not what I want to make swell."

She reached for his crotch, and he stepped back from her counter.

"Virginia, we're in your place of business."

"We could go into the back room," she said. "You remember the back room, don't you?"

He remembered her back storeroom very well. They had made love back there many times the last time he was here.

"You just have to turn the closed sign—" she started to say, but then the door opened, ringing the bell above it, and two women entered.

"Saved by the bell," she said to him.

"You'd better take care of your customers," he said.

83

"And what are you going to do?"

"I'm going outside, where it's safe."

"Coward."

He smiled at her, tipped his hat to the two ladies, and left.

"Isn't that the ruffian who shot those three poor men last night?" one of the women asked the other.

"I don't know, Madge," the second woman said. "Is it?"

"Those three *poor* men?" Virginia demanded.

Both women turned at the sound of her voice and stared at her.

"I beg your pardon?" the first one said.

"What do you mean, those three poor men?" Virginia demanded. "Three men attack one, and they're the victims?"

"Well," the first woman said, "he is a professional gunman."

"No one should have to face three guns at once, Mrs. Marley, not even a professional."

"I don't think I like your tone, Miss Madison," Mrs. Marley said.

"Well, then, why don't you take your business somewhere else?"

"But—but—" the woman stammered.

"I never!" the other woman said. "Are you going to let her speak to you that way, Madge?"

"But, Althea," Madge Marley whispered urgently, "this is the only dress shop in town."

Althea looked surprised, and then said, "You know, you're right."

"I—I do need some things . . ." Mrs. Marley said to Virginia.

"Then when you come in here," Virginia said, "I'll thank you not to talk about matters you know absolutely nothing about."

"Well . . ." Mrs. Marley said.

"Now, what can I do for you ladies?"

Clint was unaware that inside the dress shop Virginia was rushing to his aid. He decided to simply walk around town and kill some time that way.

Of course, he turned heads wherever he went, because now everyone in town knew who he was. He had the damned newspaperman to thank for that. He decided to pay the man a visit and make sure he didn't write anything else about him in his newspaper.

Even if he had to scare the wits out of him.

TWENTY-FOUR

Clint found the newspaper office in a run-down building at the north end of town. Someone had painted the name *The Rock Springs Gazette* on the window freehand, so that the letters were uneven.

As he entered he saw John Standiford on his knees underneath his press, cursing loudly.

"Goddamned machine," Standiford was saying. "Piece of goddamned junk."

"Why don't you get rid of it?" Clint asked.

Standiford reacted violently to the sound of Clint's voice. He brought his head up quickly and banged it soundly on the machine he'd been cursing.

"Ow, goddamn it!" he snapped. He got to his feet, rubbing the top of his head. "Mr. Adams, you, uh, surprised me."

"I guess so."

"What did you ask me?"

"I asked why you don't junk it if it's giving you so much trouble."

"I can't," Standiford said, "I don't have the money for a new one. You see, I'm also the only investor in this newspaper."

"Why start one here?" Clint asked. "Why not a bigger town?"

"Because I believe this will be a bigger town."

"Could it be you expect some big news to happen here?" Clint asked.

"Like what?"

"Oh, maybe a miners' strike," Clint said. "Maybe a riot."

"A riot?"

"Don't play dumb, Mr. Standiford," Clint said. "It's not becoming."

Standiford brought his hand down from the top of his head and examined it. When he was satisfied that he was not bleeding he dropped his hand to his side.

"All right," he said. "There could be some trouble with the miners and the Chinese workers."

"Well, then, write about that," Clint said. "Don't write anything more about me."

"But you're news, as well . . . uh, sir."

"I'm also the object of everyone's attention today, and I don't like it," Clint said. "I've got things to do, and I don't enjoy being on display."

"You'll excuse me for saying so, but a man of your reputation—"

"No," Clint said, cutting him off, "I will not excuse you for saying so. A man of my reputation doesn't need any more press, Mr. Standiford. If I read something else about myself in your paper, I'll be back. Do I make myself clear?"

"I know who and what you are, Mr. Adams," Standiford said, "and I must admit that you frighten me, but I am the press, and I can't allow myself to be intimidated."

Clint stared at the man for a few moments, then at the inoperable press he was standing next to. Maybe if he just left him alone he'd never get the press started again. Without the press there'd be no paper.

"I'll get it working," Standiford said, as if he could read minds. "I always do."

"I'll tell you what," Clint said. "Keep me out of your paper for a few days and I might have a story for you."

"What kind of story?"

"Murder," Clint said, "and the capture of a killer."

Standiford was interested, and his interest was able to override his fear. He grabbed a dirty rag from a nearby table and started wiping his hand.

"I'm aware that you've been asking questions about Sam Crider's murder, Mr. Adams. Am I to understand that you don't believe that the Chinese man, Lee To, did the killing?"

"Is this off-the-record, Mr. Editor?"

Standiford thought it over and then said, "For now."

"Then the answer is no, I don't think he did it."

"Why not?"

"That's a little hard to explain."

"Try me."

"He told me he didn't do it."

"And you believed him?"

"Yes."

"Why?"

"Because I was looking into his eyes when he said it."

Standiford hesitated a moment before asking his next question.

"Weren't you and Crider friends?"

"Yes, we were."

"And you want to see his killer brought to justice?"

"I do."

"And you're convinced it's not the Chinaman."

"I am."

Standiford tossed aside the rag.

"And if I keep you out of my paper, I'll get the story?" he asked.

"You will. As soon as I find the real killer, I'll let you know."

"All right," Standiford said, "you've got a deal."

He extended a hand that was still stained with ink and grease.

"If you don't mind," Clint said, "I'll pass on the handshake. Your word is good enough."

"And so is yours."

Clint nodded, turned to leave, and said, "Good luck with the press."

"And good luck to you," Standiford said.

TWENTY-FIVE

When Clint entered Rod Craig's office the man was behind his desk, as he usually was. The other man in the room was Jeff Banks, who didn't look happy.

"Clint," Craig said.

"Rod," Clint greeted. "Banks."

"I want you to know I'm not in favor of this," Banks said.

"Why not?" Clint asked. "Are you afraid of what I might find out?"

"I'm afraid you might get hurt," Banks said. "You're gonna have to go down in the mines to talk to some of these people, and you don't belong in a mine."

"I'll be on my best behavior," Clint said.

"I'm not gonna baby-sit you."

"I'm not asking you to."

Clint didn't bother telling Banks that he'd been in mines before—gold mines, not coal mines, but the principle was the same.

"Jeff will cooperate, Clint," Craig said.

"Only because you own a piece of the mine," Banks said, making his feelings clear.

"I don't care what the reason is, Jeff," Clint said. "I just want cooperation."

"And when do you want it?"

"How does now sound?"

"Bad . . . but you're the boss . . . one of them, any-way." Banks turned to Craig. "See you later, Craig."

"You're a good man, Jeff."

"Yeah, yeah," Banks said, walking past Clint and opening the door. "Well? You coming?"

"I'm coming," Clint said, and followed him out.

When they reached the mine Banks made a general announcement to the men who were gathered outside.

"This is Clint Adams," he said. "He owns a piece of the mine. I guess you all know what that means."

"We got another boss," one of the men called out.

"Just what we need," another chimed in.

"I'm not here to tell you how to do your jobs," Clint said. "Just to talk with you."

"About what?" somebody yelled.

"I think I'd like to do that one at a time."

"Well," somebody said, "if you want to talk to me you'll have to come into the mine, because that's where I'll be—for now, anyway."

Clint and Banks exchanged a glance. Both men recognized the veiled reference to the possible strike.

"Jeff," Clint said, "before I start on the men I'd like to talk to you first."

"About what?"

"Sam Crider."

"We talked about that already," Banks said. "You want to help get his killer off."

"No, I want to make sure his real killer is brought to justice."

"As far as I'm concerned, his killer is in jail right now."

"Just bear with me for a few moments, all right?"

Banks made a face and said, "You're the boss."

"Were there any of the men Sam didn't get along with?" Clint asked.

"Sure," Banks said. "He was the boss. Even though he was a good one, there were men he didn't get along with. Now if you're gonna ask me if there were any of the men who wanted to kill him, I'd have to say no."

"Did he have a violent argument with anyone a few days before he was killed?"

"Sure," Banks said again, "with me, for one, and a few of the other men. We all have violent arguments, it's part of the job. That doesn't mean I killed him."

Clint frowned. This conversation with Jeff Banks was not helping. He hoped that the conversations with the men wouldn't go like this—but he was afraid they would.

"All right," Clint said, "I guess I'd better start talking to the men."

"Talk to the ones who are outside the mine first," Banks said. "The less time you're inside, the less chance there is you'll get yourself killed."

The suggestion was sound, even if the reason wasn't.

"Thanks for the concern."

"I'm not concerned about you," Banks said, "we just can't afford any work stoppages, and if you get killed that's what would happen until we moved your body."

"I tell you what," Clint said, "if I get myself killed in the mine, just work around me. I won't mind."

Banks almost smiled in spite of himself and said, "You got a deal."

TWENTY-SIX

Clint spent the rest of the afternoon talking to men who didn't want to talk to him—especially when they found out what he wanted to talk about. Most of them hoped "that little Chink bastard hung," for what he did to Sam Crider. A few claimed not to have any feelings one way or the other, because they didn't have all the facts.

When he ran into the men he'd backed down in the saloon, one by one, they answered his questions in as few words as possible. Two of them were angry, but the other two seemed afraid to meet his eyes.

He certainly didn't get through all of the men the first day, but at least it was a start.

He stopped in at Banks's shack to tell him he was leaving.

"We still got some daylight."

"I've talked to enough men, and been inside the mine long enough. I'll continue tomorrow."

"You didn't get yourself killed," Banks said. "That surprises me."

"I'm full of surprises, Jeff."

"I'll take your word for it," Banks snapped. "I don't want to get to know you better."

"That's okay," Clint said, "I'm not here to make friends. I'm here to find out who killed Sam Crider."

Banks shook his head.

"You're so goddamned cocksure that it wasn't that Chinaman, huh?"

"Yes, I am."

"Tell me, who do you think it is?"

"I don't know."

"No suspects?"

"One or two."

"Like who?"

"Whoever had to gain from Crider's death."

"It sounds like you're talking about Rod Craig," Banks said. "He wouldn't kill his own partner—and, by the way, his friend."

"Does he gain from Sam's death?" Clint asked. "Or does he lose?"

Banks thought a moment.

"I guess he loses," Banks said. "Sam probably could have averted a strike. Now there's bound to be one."

Clint felt guilty for a moment that he hadn't discussed the strike with any of the men while speaking to them.

"But Craig wants to use the Chinese," Clint said, "and Sam didn't."

"Craig wouldn't kill Sam over that," Banks said.

"I hope you're right."

Banks frowned.

"Does Craig know you suspect him?"

"I haven't told him."

"But you're telling me," Banks said, "and maybe you're telling him that you suspect me."

"Why don't I just tell the both of you that I suspect everyone."

Banks pointed a finger at Clint.

"I still think you're looking in the wrong camp."

"I'm looking in all the camps."

"You mean you've questioned the Chinese like you have the miners?"

"That's right."

Suddenly, a light seemed to dawn on Banks.

"So that's what you were doing with that Chinese gal?" he asked. "She was your interpreter?"

"Still is, although I haven't seen her since the shooting."

"Maybe she doesn't want to see you."

"That's possible."

"What about Virginia Madison?"

"What about her?"

"Do you suspect her, too?"

"Should I?"

Banks blew some air out of his mouth, making a rude noise. "I think so."

"Why?"

"Because she was looking to get rid of Sam."

"Why?"

"Because," Banks said, "she had a new man in her life, and Sam didn't like it."

Clint frowned.

"Oh, this is news to you," Banks said.

"Who was the man?"

"I don't know that."

"Then how do you know there was one?"

"Because Sam told me."

"You and Sam were that close?"

"We were friends."

"He was friends with Rod," Clint said. "Did you tell him, too?"

Banks looked away.

"Craig was the man?" Clint asked.

"I didn't say that," Banks said. "I don't speak against my boss."

"But Sam thought it was Craig, is that what you're saying . . . by not saying it?"

"I ain't gonna talk about my boss behind his back."

"That go for me, too?" Clint asked.

Banks gave Clint a bold look.

"Craig hired me," he said. "I'm loyal to him."

"I don't have a problem with that, Jeff," Clint said. "Loyalty is a good thing. A lot of these men were loyal to Sam, I found out today, and you might be interested to know they're loyal to you."

"Is that so?"

Clint nodded.

"A few of them took offense when I asked them if you had any reason to kill Sam."

Banks shook his head.

"I don't benefit from killing, Sam," Banks said. "In my case you really better look elsewhere."

"I'm going to look elsewhere," Clint said, "and everywhere."

"Even at Virginia Madison?"

"You think Virginia is capable of bashing in the head of her man?"

"She wanted to get rid of him," Banks said. "Then again, maybe she got her lover to do it."

"So you don't think Craig was her lover?"

"I don't have any opinion," Banks said. "I just think that if you say you're gonna look everywhere, then you better look everywhere."

"You know what, Jeff," Clint said. "I think you're right."

"You do?"

"About a lot of things," Clint said, moving to the door. "I'll be back bright and early tomorrow to finish talking to the men."

"We'll be here," Banks said.

Clint opened the door and left.

TWENTY-SEVEN

Clint went back to his hotel, hoping that Virginia would not be waiting for him in his room. He had to think about what Jeff Banks had told him.

Virginia had already said that it was all over between her and Sam Crider. So what if she was seeing a man in town? Clint was going to find out who killed Sam Crider and then leave.

However, if that man was Rod Craig it shed new light on Crider's death.

But what if the man wasn't Craig?

What if it was Banks, and he had just been trying to throw Clint off the scent?

What if it was Sheriff Reasoner?

Sure, or the bartender at the saloon, Ben?

Who else would it be but, of course, Rod Craig? Craig had wanted Virginia back when she was with Clint, and then the whole time she was with Crider. He would have—should have—been waiting anxiously for a split with Crider.

But would he have wanted Virginia badly enough to kill his friend and partner? And if he did it, did Virginia help him?

When he got to his room he was relieved to find it empty. The bed was unmade, and it smelled of her. Her scent was so strong that his body began to react to it.

He went to the pitcher and basin to splash some water on his face. Forget what had gone on in that bed last night and think.

Virginia didn't say that Crider was leaving her, or that she was leaving him. She said that it had gone bad between them and was practically over. Did Crider see it that way?

It was getting dark and Clint again wondered who in this town knew everything that went on.

Why, the bartender, of course.

Clint walked to the saloon and entered. Immediately he recognized that probably half the men in the place were miners. Some of them he had even talked to. These men gave him the eye as he approached the bar, but did not make a move toward him.

"Beer, Ben," he said.

"Comin' up."

He waited for Ben to come back with the beer.

"Can you spare me a minute?" Clint said.

Ben looked around, then dropped his bar rag over his shoulder and said, "Sure. What can I do for you?"

"You probably talk to more people in this town than anyone."

Ben leaned on the bar and nodded.

"You're probably right about that."

"Did Sam Crider ever talk to you?"

"About what?"

"About anything."

"Well, yeah, sure," Ben said. "He came in here a lot, and talked about lots of things."

"Business?"

"Sure."

"His private life?"

Ben thought a moment, then said, "Probably."

"Did he go into detail?"

"I gotta tell ya," Ben said, "with the number of people who come in here and talk to me about their work and their wives and their kids, I only listen half the time."

"Ben, I'm looking for anything Crider might have told you about his partner, or his woman."

"Ah," Ben said, as if he suddenly understood. "You think Craig and Virginia were seeing each other behind his back?"

"I don't know," Clint said. "Maybe she was seeing somebody else. Did you ever hear anything about her?"

"I think Crider might have mentioned once that he didn't understand her—but doesn't every man say that about his woman?"

"Nothing more specific?"

Ben thought a moment, then shook his head and said, "No."

"What about other men talking about her?" Clint asked. "Anybody come in and brag to you about seeing her behind his back?"

Ben hesitated.

"You know," he said, "if I talked about half of what I heard—and remember, I only listen to half of what's said to me—it would probably get a lot of people killed."

"I'm not going to kill anyone, Ben," Clint said. "I'm trying to find out who killed Crider."

Ben seemed to think that over, then looked around to see if anyone else was close enough to hear what he was going to say.

"I only heard one man's name mentioned as far as Virginia Madison was concerned."

"And who was that?"

He hesitated, then said, "Jeff Banks."

"What did you hear exactly?"

"A couple of the miners were talking, and one of

them said that Banks was seeing Virginia, and he wished it was him."

"Seeing her?"

"He was a little coarser," Ben said, "if you know what I mean."

"But there was no doubt about what he meant?" Clint asked.

"No doubt," Ben said. "Now, lemme say this. There was no doubt what he meant, but I don't know how true what he said was."

"I understand."

"Don't go telling Banks you heard it from me."

"I won't," Clint promised.

Ben leaned closer.

"You think Banks did it?"

"I don't know."

"Maybe over the woman?"

"Don't know, Ben," Clint said again. "Did you ever tell this to the sheriff?"

Ben straightened up.

"What for?"

"It might have kept him from locking up Lee To," Clint said.

"I doubt it," Ben said, "but then again, he never asked me."

Why would he? Clint thought. As far as Reasoner was concerned he had the killer.

"Okay, Ben, thanks."

"Sure thing," the bartender said. "Hey, if that Chinaman really didn't kill Sam Crider, I hope you find out who did."

"Yeah," Clint said, "so do I."

TWENTY-EIGHT

Clint remained in the saloon and lingered over his beer. The place started to fill up, and soon there was no room at the bar. Every so often someone would come and try to jostle his way through to get a drink. Sometimes nobody complained, but every so often somebody would and a fight would almost result. Finally, Clint decided to give up his spot to someone else, and moved away from the bar.

He knew he could have left the saloon and gone to see Virginia. In fact, she was probably waiting for him to come to her house. It had become a routine the last time he was in town, and could easily become one again. What kept him away was the nagging question of who she had been seeing behind Crider's back, if anyone. By the time his beer was gone he'd decided the only way to really find out was to ask her—even though he risked getting her angry.

When he reached her house he saw that it was well lit from within. He went to the front door and knocked, and she answered almost immediately.

"I wondered if you were coming," she said when she answered the door. "I hoped you would."

She opened the door, made as if to kiss him, then stopped as she sensed something was wrong.

"Will you come in?" she asked.

"Yes," he said. "We have to talk, Virginia."

"More talk?"

He nodded.

"About Sam?"

He nodded again.

"All right," she said. "Come in, then, and let's get it out of the way."

She stepped aside and let him enter, then closed the door behind them. She followed him into the small living room.

"Might as well sit down," she said. "Will this take long? Shall I get coffee?"

"Let's talk first, Virginia," he said, "and then you can decide if you want me to stay long enough to have coffee."

"Oh, my," she said, "this is to be a real serious talk."

"I'm afraid so."

"You want to know if I was cheating on Sam?"

He looked surprised.

"It wasn't that hard to figure, Clint."

He waited a moment, then said, "Well . . . were you?"

"We weren't married."

"That doesn't answer the question."

"Doesn't it?"

"We're not going to get anywhere this way."

"And where do we want to get to?" she asked.

"I want to know if you were cheating, and if so, who with?"

"And what will that mean to you and me?"

"Nothing," he said, "at least, not to me. We're not married, either, and I wasn't here then. I don't know what it will mean to you. Maybe you'll be angry at me for prying."

"I would be," she said, "if I didn't know that you were still trying to figure out who killed him."

She fell silent then, and he had to prompt her.

"Well?"

"Was I cheating?"

He nodded.

"I did," she said, "I did cheat on him, yes."

"With who?"

"With no one who would kill him."

"Virginia . . ."

She sighed, rubbed her hand over her forehead.

"I told you that sex with him wasn't . . . satisfying, right?"

He nodded.

"Well . . . I thought I deserved to be satisfied."

He remained silent.

"So I went looking."

"And?"

"I looked . . . in more than one place."

"You mean, you cheated with more than one man?"

"Yes."

"How many?"

She hesitated, then said, "Six."

"Six men?"

"Over a six-month period," she hastened to add.

"I'm not judging you, Virginia."

"I feel like you are," she said.

"I'm not."

"I'm not a slut."

"I know you're not."

She looked away.

"Then why do I feel like one?"

"Because you're judging yourself."

"I guess so."

"We can go on with this without me judging you, Virginia. Maybe you can even take it easy on yourself, all right?"

She nodded and said, "All right."

TWENTY-NINE

"Of these six men," Clint continued, "did you see any of them more than once?"

"Two of them."

"And were any of them . . . serious about you?"

"Yes."

"How many?"

"Three."

"So there are four men who you only slept with once, right? With no involvement?"

"Right."

"Well . . . maybe we can eliminate them," Clint said. "Did they try to come back for more?"

"Three are married," she said, "and all three knew that it was only going to happen once. Besides, it wasn't very satisfying with them, either, so I didn't want to go back."

"And the other three?"

"Another one was only once, but he kept coming around wanting more," she said. "I didn't. After a while he got the message."

"And who was that?" This was the big moment, when he started asking for names.

"I'm not proud of this, Clint."

"I know."

"His name's Martin James—Marty. He was—he is eighteen years old."

Clint tried to keep his amusement from showing, but he couldn't.

"Don't laugh at me," she said.

"I'm not," he said. "If he was that young I guess he fell in love with you."

"For a while," she said, "but he got over it."

"Are you sure?"

"Yes," she said. "It was months ago, and he doesn't even speak to me when we pass on the street. His mother is a customer of mine."

"I see."

"You're still amused," she said accusingly.

"But not laughing," he said. "All right, you know I have to ask. Who were the other two? The ones you've been with more than once?"

She rubbed her hands together and looked away.

"Shall I guess?" he asked.

She didn't answer.

"Jeff Banks and Rod Craig?"

She hesitated, then said, "Banks, yes, but not Rod."

"Really?"

"Does that surprise you?"

"Frankly, yes."

"Well, it's not like Rod didn't make it clear to me all the time that he wanted me."

"How long did it last with Banks?"

"A month," she said. "We saw each other half a dozen times."

"It was satisfying with him?"

"No," she said, "but I thought I could . . . make it be, eventually."

"But it wasn't."

"No."

"So you called it off."

"Yes."

"How did he take it?"

"Not well."

"He was angry?"

"Angry," she said. "Hurt. He thought I was going to break it off with Sam for him."

"Was he mad enough to kill Sam?"

"Mad enough to kill me, maybe," she said, "but I don't think Sam."

"So who was the other one, Virginia?" he asked. "The sixth man?"

She hesitated again, licked her lips, and said, "Nobody you know."

"Then why don't you want to tell me?"

"Because when Sam was killed," she said, "I was still seeing him."

"Do you think he did it?"

"I . . . don't know."

"Are you still seeing him?"

"Not since . . ." She looked him straight in the eye then for the first time since they'd started talking. "Not since you came to town."

"And how has he taken that?"

"Not well."

"So he's in love with you."

"Yes."

"And wanted you to leave Sam?"

"Yes."

"And the sex . . ."

"Was good," she said. "Not like with you, but better than the others."

"So . . . were you going to leave Sam for him?"

"I hadn't decided yet when Sam . . . was killed."

"So, maybe he killed Sam to help you decide," Clint said.

Virginia didn't say anything.

"I think I have to talk to him, Virginia."

"I know."

"Is he married?" Clint asked. "Is there a wife in the picture?"

"No."

"So who is he?"

"He's a miner," she said. "His name is Michael Garrett."

"He worked for Sam?"

She nodded.

"How'd you meet him?" This was just idle curiosity.

"I just happened to go by the office one day to see Sam, and Mike was there. We saw each other and . . . that night we had sex. It just . . . happened."

Clint knew how that worked. An instant attraction between two people was something that's hard to resist. Maybe that was one of the reasons he'd never committed himself to one woman. If he did, what would happen when that instant attraction happened again? Would he be able to resist? He was probably always afraid to find out.

"Does that sound terrible?" she asked.

"No," Clint said. "In fact, I was just thinking how I could understand it."

"I know," she said. "It happened that way with us, didn't it?"

"Yes, it did."

"But with us," she said, "it never wore off, did it, Clint?"

"No." Until the day he left town that attraction had been there—and it was there when he came back.

"What about with Garrett?" Clint asked. "It must have still been there with him if you were seeing him at the time of Sam's death."

"I think it was wearing off," she said. "It's just that it was better with him than with Sam."

"Why was it wearing off?"

"He's . . . not the kind of man who treats a woman well."

Clint went cold.

"You mean he beat you?"

"I mean I think he would have," she said, "if the bruises wouldn't have given us away. I think if I left Sam for him, within a week I would have been bruised. He's kind of . . . brutal."

"And he's a miner, you said?"

"Well . . ."

"What?"

"He worked for the company," she said, "but I got the feeling he worked for Rod, and not Sam."

"And you had the feeling he wasn't a miner?"

She nodded.

"He was always too . . . clean, if you know what I mean."

"So you never asked him what he did for Rod?"

"No," she said, "I never did."

"Well," Clint said thoughtfully, "maybe I should think about asking him."

THIRTY

Questioning Mike Garrett would not look out of place because Clint had planned to question some more of the miners the next day, anyway.

Although neither was angry with one another, Clint decided not to stay the night at Virginia's. As he left he wasn't sure he would be back. Anger had nothing to do with it.

He toyed with the idea of going back to the saloon but decided against it. Instead he headed straight back to his hotel.

He was crossing the street with his hotel just ahead of him when the first bullet kicked up the dirt at his feet. He sprang into action, hitting the ground just as the second bullet hit the dirt, as well. He rolled and kept rolling until he hit something, and two more shots were fired, which also missed. From the gap between shots it was apparent that one person was firing, probably with a rifle—one shot, then working the lever of the rifle, then another shot, and so on.

He hit a horse trough, stopped, and slid his gun from his holster. Suddenly it was quiet. He was two blocks from the saloon, and with the noise being made inside, the shots had probably gone unnoticed. At this time of night probably most of the people in town who were awake were in the saloon. Sleeping people might not notice the shots, and the buildings surrounding the hotel were businesses anyway, and closed up tight for the night.

The result was silence as Clint waited to see what would happen next. More than likely the shots had come from high up, either a hotel room on the second floor or the roof of the hotel. He decided waiting wasn't his best course of action. Instead, he got to his feet and sprinted for the hotel.

As he entered the lobby, gun in hand, he frightened the clerk, who had been on his way to the door to see what the commotion was about.

"Anybody come through the lobby in the past few minutes?" he demanded.

"Uh, no," the startled man said, "no one."

"Anyone come in and out in the last hour or so? Anyone strange?"

"Strange?"

"Anyone not registered?"

"No," the clerk said, "not that I saw. Wha—"

The clerk started to ask a question, but Clint was no longer there to answer. He ran up the stairs to the second floor and looked up and down the hall. Should he knock on each door that overlooked the street? Or kick the doors in? Or would the shooter be gone by now? Or be bold enough to simply stay in his room?

Clint heard someone behind him on the stairs and turned to see Sheriff Reasoner coming up.

"What's going on?" the lawman demanded.

"Somebody took some shots at me on the street," Clint said. "They either came from this floor or from the roof."

"Have you checked the roof yet?"

"No."

"I'll do that," Reasoner said. "There are back stairs here. Why don't you check them?"

"Okay."

"I'll meet you in the lobby."

"Fine."

They split up and Clint went down the hall the way the sheriff had pointed and found the back stairs. He went down them slowly, because they were dark, and when he reached the bottom found himself in a dark hallway. He took out a lucifer match and struck it, giving meager light to the area. He moved forward until he reached the back door, which was locked from the inside. Whoever the shooter was, he hadn't gone out this way—or, if he had, someone had locked the door behind him.

He turned and looked for a way to the lobby from where he was, so he wouldn't have to go back upstairs. He found a hallway and followed it. He came out behind the desk, frightening the clerk again.

"Jesus," the man said, putting his hand to his heart.

"Sorry," Clint said, moving around the desk.

"What's going on?"

"Somebody took shots at me," Clint said, "probably from somewhere inside the hotel."

"I haven't seen anybody," the clerk said, shaking his head.

"Probably somebody in one of the front rooms. Who's in those rooms?"

"Uh . . ." the clerk started, but he stopped as the sheriff came down the stairs.

"Nobody on the roof," Reasoner said.

"I was just asking the desk clerk who was in the front rooms."

"Good question," Reasoner said, and looked pointedly at the clerk.

"Uh, I'll have to look at the register . . ." the clerk stammered, reaching for it.

"We can do that," Reasoner said, and grabbed the book first.

"Front rooms . . ."

"There are four," the clerk said. "One, two, eleven, and twelve."

"One," the sheriff said, "Flanders, William. Denver, Colorado."

"A drummer," the clerk said.

"What's he look like?" Clint asked.

"Fat, fifty," the clerk said. "Sweats a lot."

"Two," Reasoner said, "Creston, Mary."

"Temperance lady," the clerk said. "She's gonna save Rock Springs."

"Not tonight," the sheriff said. "Eleven. Clark, Herman."

"Preacher," the clerk said.

"He's gonna save Rock Springs, too?" Clint asked.

"He stays in his room every night and gets drunk," the clerk said.

"He's having a faith crisis," the sheriff said. Then he looked at Clint. "Twelve's empty."

"That's right," the clerk said. "They checked out this morning."

"Let's check it," Reasoner said, closing the book. "Key," he said to the clerk, who handed it over. He and Clint went back to the stairs.

THIRTY-ONE

They reached the door and stopped to listen at it. It was quiet.

"How do you want to do this?" Clint asked.

"We'll have to do it quick," Reasoner whispered. "I'll put the key in as quiet as I can, turn it, and then we'll go in fast."

"Who first?"

"Me."

"Okay."

Reasoner slid the key into the lock carefully, then suddenly turned it and opened the door. He went in first, and then Clint followed, thinking how unfair it was that he was being shielded by the sheriff's big body.

Clint moved out from behind the sheriff as soon as he could so he could cover part of the room with his gun, but there was no need.

"Empty," Reasoner said, looking around.

Clint walked to the window and looked down.

"This is where he was, all right," he said, stooping to pick up ejected rifle shells from the floor. There were four and he handed them to the sheriff.

"A Winchester."

"Winchester ammo, anyway," Clint said.

Reasoner jingled the shells in his hand.

"How did he get out of the hotel?" he asked.

"Maybe he didn't."

"You think he might still be here? In one of the other rooms?"

"Maybe."

"We can get the keys to all the rooms and check."

"What good would that do? He'd act like we woke him up, just like all the others."

"That's true."

"He missed," Clint said, "and that's what counts."

"Do you think this has something to do with your questions?" Reasoner asked.

"Don't you?"

"Well . . . you do have a reputation."

"No," Clint said, "this is like the others. This makes me even more sure that I'm right about Sam's murder, and it should convince you, too."

"I can't just let the Chinaman go, Adams."

"I understand," Clint said, "but when the judge comes to town you can back my story."

"Sure," Reasoner said. "I can't deny that some-body's been trying to kill you since you got here, but it'll be up to the judge to decide if he believes it's be-cause of Sam or because of your reputation."

"No argument," Clint said. "Thanks for the help here tonight."

"Don't mention it."

"How'd you happen to hear the shots?"

"I was on my rounds . . . and if we're done here, I guess I'll continue them."

"And I guess I'll go to my room and turn in."

"You can sleep after this?"

Clint smiled and said, "Not without some precautions first."

THIRTY-TWO

Clint woke the next morning and checked the pitcher and basin perched on the chair he had pushed up against the door before he went to sleep. They were still there, still precariously perched so that the slightest pressure on the door would send them crashing to the floor.

He got out of bed and carefully took them from the chair to the dresser. The pitcher still had water in it, so he poured some into the basin and washed up before dressing. He strapped on his gun and went downstairs for breakfast.

In the dining room, eating his breakfast, he looked around at the other diners, wondering if any of them was the shooter. Many of them seemed to be watching him, but that had been going on ever since he killed the three men in the street.

He decided to ignore the stares of the other diners and concentrate on his own meal, and on his plans for the day.

He had many more miners to question, and in fact he had not yet finished questioning the people in the Chinese camps. But the person he most wanted to see today was, of course, Mike Garrett, Virginia's most recent lover.

He was trying to decide whether to ask Jeff Banks to

point the man out, or Rod Craig, when Craig himself appeared in the doorway of the dining room. There could be no doubt who he was looking for, so Clint made it easy for him and waved.

"Good morning," Clint said. "Coffee?"

"Yeah," Craig said, "I could use it."

Clint waved the waiter over and asked for another cup. When it arrived Clint poured it full.

"Thanks."

"Anything else, sir?" the waiter asked.

"No," Craig said to the man, "go away."

Insulted, the waiter withdrew.

"I hate waiters," Craig said. "I want them to bring me my food and then disappear until I call for them."

"Somebody got up on the wrong side of the bed this morning," Clint said.

"No," Craig said, "I've always hated waiters."

"How about waitresses?"

"I can tolerate pretty ones," Craig said, "but that's about it."

"What brings you here this morning, Rod? Besides insulting my waiter so that he'll probably spit in my food from now on before he serves it to me."

Craig sipped some coffee and then put the cup down and forgot about it.

"The strike."

"What about it?"

"It's gonna happen."

"Today?"

"Maybe not today," he said, "but in the next few days for sure."

"Why do you say that?"

"While you were talking to the miners yesterday, a representative came to see me."

"And?"

"He made it clear that either I meet their demands in

the next few days or that's it, they're striking."

"And what did you say?"

"I told him to go screw himself."

"In those words?"

"In exactly those words."

"I think I see now why Sam dealt with the miners," Clint said.

"I'm gonna talk to the Chinese today," Craig said. "I was wondering if you'd come with me."

"Why?"

"You know them."

"I know one of them."

"That's one more than I do."

Clint thought a moment, then said, "I don't know, Rod."

"Don't know about what?"

"Hiring the Chinese."

"We already have Chinese workers," Craig said. "All I'm gonna do is hire more."

"Yeah," Clint said, "as strikebreakers."

"So? They'll get paid."

"Which is all they care about," Clint said. "But do they know what might happen to them?"

"See?" Craig said. "I need you for that. You can make sure they do know, so this time nobody can say they weren't told."

Craig's argument suddenly made sense. Clint could explain the situation to Jean, so she could explain it to the others before they made their final decision.

"Okay," he said, "I'll come along."

"Good," Craig said, "thanks. I'd like to get it done this morning."

"Just let me finish my coffee."

"Oh, yeah," Craig said, reminded of his. He picked it up, sipped it, and put it back down.

"Who was the representative who spoke to you yesterday?'' Clint asked. ''Anyone I talked to already?''

''I don't think so,'' Craig said. ''This fella has worked for us from the beginning. He's a good worker, but he's kind of a troublemaker. A hardhead, you know?''

''Who is he?'' Clint asked again.

''Nobody you know,'' Craig said, ''I'm sure of it. His name's Mike Garrett.''

THIRTY-THREE

Clint and Craig walked to the end of town and on to the point where the Chinese camps started. The first one they came to was the one where Jean and her people stayed, and as they entered someone started to chatter aloud in Chinese and Jean appeared from one of the tents. She was clad in the black, roomy pajama type clothing the Chinese preferred.

"I thought you left town," she said, putting her hands on her hips.

"Not hardly," he said. "There's been too much happening. Jean, this is Rod Craig. He runs the mines."

"I know who Mr. Craig is," she said. "Why is he here?"

"Maybe I'd better let him tell you that," Clint said.

"Mr. Craig?"

"You speak very good English," Craig said.

"I understand it well, if you will speak slowly to me. Yes?"

"All right."

"Also, I will have to translate for my father and uncle. They must understand what is going on. They are the elders, and will tell the others what to do."

"Okay," Craig said. "Where are they?"

"Come."

Clint and Craig followed Jean back into the tent she

123

had come out of. Inside her father and uncle were sitting with teacups in front of them.

"Will you have tea, gentlemen?" Jean asked them.

"No, thank you," Clint said, and Craig refused also.

"Please," she said, "excuse me while I tell them why you are here."

"Sure."

She and her uncle and father conversed in Chinese for a few moments, and then she turned back to Craig.

"They are ready to hear what you have to say."

Clint stepped aside and listened to the conversation. Basically, Craig told Jean he wanted to hire her people now—hundreds of them—so that when the miners struck they would already be in place to work. She, in turn, translated this for her elders, who then replied, and she translated for Craig.

"My people will be in danger from the miners," she said when he finished.

"They'll be getting paid good money."

"How good?"

Again, Clint listened while the two dickered. Craig named a figure, Jean translated, rejected it, he named another, she translated, and they went on like that for some time until finally Jean nodded and said, "It is done."

"Can you report for work today?"

"No," she said, shaking her head. "It will take time to gather our people."

"Tomorrow morning, then?"

She asked her uncle and father, then said to Craig, "Yes."

"Good," he said, "come to the mine early tomorrow morning and I'll hand you all over to the foreman."

"We will be there."

"Jean," Clint said, "do your father and uncle—do you—properly understand the danger you might be in?"

"We understand that we will be getting paid," she said. "That is all we need to know."

Clint shrugged and said, "All right, then. I guess we're done here."

"I'll see your people tomorrow," Craig said.

"I will be there, as well, Mr. Craig. Some of the others will be women, as well. Is that a problem?"

"Not if they do their jobs," Craig said.

"They will."

"See you in the morning, then."

Jean executed a slight bow, which Craig didn't know what to do with. Clint and Craig left the camp and headed back into town.

THIRTY-FOUR

"What are you thinking?" Craig asked as they reached town.

"Somebody took some shots at me last night."

Craig stopped walking and looked at Clint.

"Where?"

"In front of my hotel."

Craig looked him over and said, "Obviously, you weren't hurt."

"No, I wasn't."

"Did you catch the shooter?"

"No," Clint said. "The sheriff showed up and we looked through the hotel, but we didn't find him."

"Did it ever occur to you," Craig asked, "to leave town?"

"No," Clint said, "not until I find out who killed Sam."

"I still think it was the Chinaman."

"Then who's been trying to get rid of me?" Clint asked. "And why?"

Craig shrugged and said, "There could be any number of reasons."

"Name one."

"Well . . . Virginia."

"What about her?"

"You've started up with her again, haven't you?"

Clint hesitated just a moment before he said, "Not exactly."

"Well," Craig said, "if you have I don't blame you, but the truth of the matter is she was seeing other men behind Sam's back."

"You know that for a fact?"

"Oh, yes."

"How?"

"Jeff Banks," Craig said. "He was one of them."

"And you?"

Craig smiled and said, "I wish. No, not me."

"So you think whoever she was seeing when I got here is trying to get rid of me?"

"That's one possible answer, isn't it?"

"Sure," Clint said, "it's possible. Do you know who that might be?"

"No," Craig said, "I don't know who the latest is."

"Rod, I'd still like to do something to try to avert the strike."

"What can you do?"

"Would you introduce me to this Mike Garrett and let me talk to him?"

"Sure," Craig said. "You want to do that now?"

"No time like the present."

"Let's go to the mine, then."

"Lead on."

THIRTY-FIVE

Craig allowed Clint to wait in his office while he went and got Mike Garrett. This was his way of saying thanks for going to the Chinese camps with him. When the door opened it was Mike Garrett who stepped in, without Rod Craig.

"Mike Garrett?" Clint asked, just to make sure.

"That's right."

Garrett was a muscular man with dark, curly hair and big hands. He had powerful shoulders and upper arms, which would serve him well as a miner.

"My name's Clint Adams."

Garrett looked surprised.

"The boss said I had to talk to you, but he didn't tell me who you were."

"Is that a problem?"

"Naw," Garrett said with a shrug, "not if it isn't for you."

"Why would it be for me?"

Garrett smiled, revealing well cared for teeth. He had a smile that would make women swoon.

"I think we both know why I'm here."

"And why's that?"

"Virginia Madison," Garrett said. "Does Craig know about her?"

"What about her?"

"We gonna play games?" Garrett asked. "If this is gonna take that long maybe I better sit down."

"Go ahead," Clint said, "have a seat," and he himself sat behind Craig's desk.

Garrett took a chair directly across from Clint and adopted an arrogant pose.

"I'm not here to talk about Virginia," Clint said. "What you and she do is your business."

"Her and me ain't doin' nothin' since you got to town," Garrett said, and then surprised Clint by saying, "but that's all right."

"Is it?"

"Oh, sure," Garrett said with a shrug, " 'cause you're gonna leave town eventually, and me and her will still be here. She'll come lookin' for me then."

"That'll be nice for you," Clint said. "Actually, I'm only interested in your relationship with Virginia as it affected Sam Crider's life . . . and death."

Garrett sat up straighter.

"I didn't kill him," he said. "They got a Chinaman in jail who killed him."

"Lee To didn't kill Crider."

"Who says?"

"He does," Clint said, "and I do."

Garrett frowned and looked at Clint suspiciously.

"So you're lookin' for somebody else to pin it on?" he asked.

"Sam Crider was my friend," Clint said. "I'm going to find out who killed him, and I'm going to make that person pay."

"I didn't kill him," Garrett said. "Is that what Virginia told you?"

"No."

"What'd she say, then, that bitch?" Garrett asked. "She sic you on me?"

"She told me about you and her."

"She tell you about her and all the other men?"

"Yes."

"Everybody knew about her."

"Did Sam?"

Garrett snorted. "He was blind, or he only saw what he wanted to see."

"So then he didn't know about her and other men?"

"I can't say that for sure," he said. "I worked for him, but I didn't know him well."

"What about somebody else, Garrett?"

"What do you mean?"

"I mean if you were going to pick somebody who you thought had a reason to kill Sam Crider, or who might have killed him, who would it be?"

"You want me to point the finger at somebody else for you?" Garrett asked. "I ain't gonna do that."

"Not even to get yourself off the hook?"

"I work with these guys," Garrett said. "They all trust me. I wouldn't do that to them—not to any of them."

"That kind of loyalty to your friends is commendable, Mike. Can I call you Mike?"

"I don't care what you call me, Adams, as long as you don't try to pin Crider's murder on me."

"So you wouldn't have killed him to get Virginia for yourself?"

"Why should I kill a man to get something I can have anytime I want, anyway?"

"You mean you could have gotten her to leave Sam?"

Garrett snorted. "Anytime," he said. "You know what Virginia is, Adams. You know what she likes. You gave it to her, I gave it to her. Sam Crider never could. Don't get me wrong. I think Crider was a hell of a man, I really do. I respected him as my boss. He just couldn't give Virginia what she wanted.'' Garrett leaned forward. ''Not the way you and me can.''

''Is that a fact?''

''It is a fact,'' Garrett said. ''Just ask Virginia.''

Clint stared at Garrett long enough for the man to start to squirm.

''Are we done talkin' about this?'' Garrett asked.

Clint hesitated, then said, ''Yeah . . . for now.''

Garrett got up to leave.

''Don't leave.''

Garrett stopped in the act of heading for the door.

''I thought we were through.''

''We are,'' Clint said, ''that is, talking about Sam and Virginia.''

Garrett frowned and asked, ''Then what—''

''Sit down,'' Clint said. ''Let's talk about this strike.''

THIRTY-SIX

Talking with Mike Garrett about the strike was a lot harder than discussing Sam Crider's murder, or his relationship with Virginia. For one thing, Clint found himself agreeing with Garrett. The demands he was making for his men sounded reasonable: more money—but not that much more; more and shorter shifts, which would not affect the total number of hours a miner worked; also, more safety precautions; and they wanted some housing, so that some of them could move their families to Rock Springs.

All of these things seemed fair to Clint.

"Craig won't give in on any of this?"

Garrett shook his head.

"Not one item."

"And Sam was going to?"

"Sam saw the sense of it, Adams," Garrett said. "He was trying to talk Craig into at least some of it, enough so that we could make a deal without either side really giving in."

"It's an ego thing."

"Sure, ego has a lot to do with it," Garrett said, "but we just want what's fair. You can see that, can't you?"

"Yes," Clint said, "as a matter of fact, Mike, I can."

"Then you'll talk to him?"

"I will, but can you give me more time?"

133

With that Garrett stood up and shook his head.

"I'm sorry," Garrett said, "but we've waited long enough already. Tomorrow, unless he gives in to at least some of our demands, we're going on strike—all except the Chinese."

"Why won't the Chinese strike?"

"They're not with us," Garrett said. "And a lot of them already have their families living in their camps, in tents. We won't bring our wives and children here to live in tents."

"You have a wife and children, Mike?"

Garrett looked away, realizing he'd given out information he'd rather not have shared.

"Yeah," he said, "I've got a wife and two kids."

"And you want to bring them here?"

"Yeah."

"Does Virginia know this?"

"Yeah, she knows," Garrett said.

And suddenly, just like that—as long as he was telling the truth, and Clint had the feeling he was—Mike Garrett's motive to murder Sam Crider went right out the window.

"There ain't that many Chinese in the mines, though," Garrett went on, backtracking a bit. "They won't be able to keep up productivity."

"Mike," Clint said, "there are plenty of Chinese willing to work the mines." He didn't bother to tell the man that Craig had hired hundreds of them just that morning.

"You tell that son of a bitch," Garrett snapped, pointing a finger at Clint, "that if he brings in Chinese scabs he's gonna have a war on his hands."

Garrett stormed to the door and opened it.

"You tell him that!" he shouted and stalked out.

There were several miners waiting outside the building for Mike Garrett.

"So?" one asked.

"Does he listen any better than Craig?" another demanded.

"He's a lot like Sam Crider was," Garrett said. "He's fair, and he's gonna talk to Craig."

"Did you give in?" one of them asked. "He must have asked for more time."

"He did, and I told him no. Unless some of our demands are met, we strike tomorrow."

"And what about the Chinamen?"

"I told him that if Craig brings in Chinese scabs, we go to war."

"All right," one of them said, while another shouted, "Yeah!"

Garrett turned and looked back at the building and shook his head. He knew in his heart the strike was going to happen. As he followed his coworkers back to camp, he wasn't even thinking about Sam Crider or Virginia Madison.

THIRTY-SEVEN

Clint looked up as the office door opened about ten minutes later and Rod Craig walked in.

"Can I have my desk back?" he asked, closing the door behind him.

"It's all yours."

Clint got up and came around one side of the desk while Craig went around the other.

"How did it go with Garrett?"

"It was interesting."

"Oh, yeah? I don't like the sound of that."

"Why? Because I might agree with some of their demands?"

"I knew it," Craig said, sitting back in his chair. "You're just like Sam. You're buying into their demands."

"Some of them are reasonable, Rod," Clint said. "In fact, a lot of them are."

"Like housing? So they can bring their families?"

"What's wrong with that?"

"Because families take time away from the mines, that's what," Craig said. "How many times do you think a miner is going to come in here and need a day off for the wifey or the kiddies?"

"You're not much of a family man, are you, Rod?" Clint asked.

"They're too much damn trouble. They take away from the work."

"Well, you know, to some of these men their families are more important than their work."

"That's my point, exactly. And how about that bit about shorter shifts?"

"Seems to me the men wouldn't tire out as much by the end of their shift."

"Why do I care how tired they are at the end of their shift?" Craig demanded. "They're finished, aren't they? They can go lie down someplace, can't they?"

"Rod," Clint said, "if you don't start to change your attitude you're going to have that strike on your hands tomorrow."

"I've got workers coming here tomorrow, remember?" Craig said. "That's all I'm worried about."

Clint stared at Craig and suddenly knew what Sam Crider must have been going through, and he'd had a lot more time to work on the man. There was no way Clint was going to change his mind overnight.

"You'd better be prepared for what's going to happen tomorrow, Rod."

"I'm prepared to get our work done tomorrow, that's what I'm prepared for."

Clint left the office knowing a lot more than that was going to happen tomorrow.

THIRTY-EIGHT

Clint went right from the mine to the sheriff's office. Reasoner was seated behind his desk, looking tired.

"Didn't sleep well last night?" Clint asked.

"I ain't gonna sleep well until that damned judge gets here," the lawman said. "What brings you here?"

"I thought I'd warn you."

"About what?"

Briefly, he told Reasoner what he thought was going to happen tomorrow.

"What's that got to do with me?" the sheriff asked. "Seems to me that's more Rod Craig's problem than mine."

"Sheriff," Clint said, "if there's a riot it could turn into one hell of a bloodbath."

"You really think there'll be a riot?"

"If Craig's Chinese workers go into the mines tomorrow morning while the white workers are on strike outside? What do you think?"

"Still," Reasoner said, "it's outside of town."

"I understand you said you were still learning this job," Clint said. "It's not that far outside of town."

"All right," Reasoner said, "what would you suggest I do?"

"Get some men over to the mines tomorrow morning for when the Chinese workers show up."

"I don't have any men, Adams," Reasoner said. "I have no deputies."

"Get some."

"Just like that?"

"Assign some," Clint said. "Go out today and find yourself some men."

"That's not gonna be easy in this town," Reasoner said. "It's not exactly filled with people who are that civic-minded. Besides, once they find out it's for the mine . . ." He shook his head.

"So you're not even going to try?"

"Oh," Reasoner said, "I'll try . . ."

But the man obviously wasn't very optimistic about his chances.

"What about you?" the sheriff asked. "You want to wear a deputy's star?"

"I'll be there, anyway," Clint said. "I don't need to wear a star."

"See?" Reasoner said, as if Clint's reaction explained it all.

"No," Clint said, opening the door, "I don't see."

He left without further word.

Craig looked across his desk at the man.

"It's got to be done tonight, and done right," he said, "or he's gonna get in my way tomorrow."

"All right," the man said, "I'll do it myself."

"Who took those shots at him last night?"

"It was me."

"And you missed?"

"It was dark," the man said, "and he moves real fast."

"Jesus . . ." Craig said, shaking his head. "You know, if he finds out, I won't go to jail. He'll just kill me himself."

"He's that loyal to his friends?"

"Yes."

"Guess you don't know what that's like, huh?"

"Crider was my partner," Craig spat back. "I never claimed we were friends."

"No," the other man said, "he was the one who said that."

"That was his problem," Craig said. "I've got another job for you."

"What's that?"

"Mike Garrett."

"What about him?"

"I want him dead, too."

"This is gonna get expensive for you."

Craig scowled.

"Just do it. Without him around tomorrow I can stave off trouble."

"You mean they won't strike without him?"

"No," Craig said, "I mean they won't slaughter the Chinese without him."

THIRTY-NINE

When Clint got back to his hotel he was surprised to find Jean waiting for him in the lobby. This fact did not seem to sit well with the clerk, who was frowning at her as Clint entered.

"Hello," Clint said. "Waiting for me?"

"Yes," she said, rising from the sofa she was sitting on. "I want to talk to you."

"Would you like something to eat?" Clint asked. "We could go into the dining room."

She looked toward the dining room, then at Clint, shaking her head.

"I cannot go in there."

"Why not?"

"They would not allow it."

"You can go in there with me," he said, and started for the doorway. She reached out and grabbed his arm in both her hands, stopping him.

"No, I do not wish to go in there."

"Well," Clint said, "if you don't want to go in that's different. Where would you like to go?"

"To your room."

Clint looked surprised.

"You would feel safe with me in my room, Jean?" he asked her.

She nodded.

"I would feel safer with you there than I would . . . in there," she said, jerking her chin toward the dining room.

"All right, then," Clint said with a smile, "we'll go to my room."

Clint unlocked the door and let her go in, then closed it behind them.

"Sit down, Jean, and tell me what I can do for you," he said.

She looked around the room, as if she had never been in a hotel room before, and maybe she hadn't.

"Would you like to wash your hands and face?" he asked. He noticed that her hands were grimy, and there were a few dirt marks on her face. Also, her clothes were dirty. Of course, this came from living in a camp where the only shelter was a tent, with a dirt floor.

"There's water in that pitcher," he said, drawing her attention to the dresser top. "I can pour some into that basin and you can wash, if you want. Do you?"

She hesitated a moment, then said, "Yes, please."

Clint walked over and poured the water into the basin, then stepped aside. Jean stood up and walked slowly to the dresser.

"How long has it been since you've had a bath?" he asked her.

"I bathe in the stream."

"I mean a real bath, in a tub."

She thought a moment, then shook her head.

"I do not remember."

"We can go downstairs and get you a bath."

"No," she said quickly.

"They won't refuse you if you're with me," he assured her.

"No," she said, "this will be good enough."

She dipped her hands into the water and let it run through her fingers for a moment.

"Here," he said, handing her a bar of soap. "And let's roll these up so they don't get wet." He undid the sleeves of the dirty man's shirt that was too big for her and rolled up the sleeves.

"Okay," he said, "go ahead."

He watched as she lathered her hands and washed the dirt off them, then cupped the water in her hands and lifted it to her face. The way she was doing it—almost reverently—told him that she was enjoying it.

And then she did something that totally surprised him. She started to unbutton her shirt.

"Jean . . ."

"I want to feel the water, here," she said, touching her chest, "on my body."

"But . . ."

She finished unbuttoning the shirt, took it off, and dropped it to the floor. He couldn't help but stare. She had a beautiful body, her breasts small but firm and round, with brown nipples, and her skin was lovely. She wet her hands, then pressed them to her breasts, closing her eyes.

"Here," he said, and when she opened her eyes he handed her a washcloth.

She wet the cloth and rubbed it over her torso. The feel of the cloth on her nipples made them hard, or maybe it was a chill that caused it.

When she was done he handed her a towel and she gently dried herself, then turned to him, seemingly unmindful of her nakedness.

"Do you think I am pretty?" she asked.

"I think you're very pretty," he said.

She patted herself dry a few more times, then tossed the towel aside. She lifted her eyes to his and boldly held his gaze.

"I . . . I . . . do not know how to say what I want," she told him.

"That's all right," he said. "I think I know. If I'm wrong, you tell me, all right?"

"All right."

He stepped to her and palmed her breasts. They filled his hands like peaches.

"Am I wrong?" he asked.

She smiled and said, "No, you are not wrong."

FORTY

He put his arms around her and drew her to him. She slid her hands inside his shirt, and her palms were hot on his skin. Slowly, she unbuttoned his shirt and kissed his chest. She was much shorter than he was and he had to lean down to kiss her, but it was worth it. Her mouth was sweet, timid at first, then avid.

He turned her, backed her up to the bed, and pushed her down on it. Her eyes were shining as he pulled off her shoes, then undid her pants and slid them off. When she was completely naked he stared at her for a few moments, then started to undress. Her eyes watched him hungrily, and when he was naked and she saw his rigid penis they widened.

Clint put one knee on the bed and slid his hand over her belly. She gasped as his hand traveled upward and played with her nipples. He brought his other knee up onto the bed on the other side of her and straddled her. He leaned down to kiss, lick, and suck her breasts, and as he did so he rubbed his penis over her belly. She moaned, moved her legs, then reached down to grasp him.

"No," she said, "you must be inside me now . . ."

"No," he said, "wait," and pulled away from her grasp.

He got on his knees in front of the bed and began to

kiss her legs and thighs. She instinctively knew where he was headed and she quickly crossed her legs and said, "No."

"You don't like that?" he asked. "You don't like to be kissed . . . here?" He put his hand over her vagina.

"I am not clean."

He smiled at her.

"We can fix that."

He went to the dresser for the basin of water and the washcloth. He looked around for someplace to dump the dirty water, then decided to open the window and dump it in the alley. After that he poured clean water into it and carried it to the bed.

He knelt again and gently began to wash her. He started at her feet, then her ankles, calves, and thighs, and then between her legs.

"You have to open yourself to me so I can do this," he said.

"I have done this to men before," she said, "but it has never been done to me."

"Well," he said, "there's always a first time. Spread your legs for me, Jean . . ."

"Yes," she said, and spread them.

Very gently he put the washcloth to her vagina and began to rub, and clean. He used one finger beneath the cloth and gradually began to rub her harder and faster. Suddenly, washing her got lost, and she gasped and opened her legs even wider as he "cleaned" her. He continued to manipulate her with his finger beneath the cloth, kissing her thighs, and then her belly, then moving up onto the bed with her and kissing her breasts. He tossed the washcloth away and began to touch her without it. He slid his fingers up and down her until she was good and wet, and then dipped two fingers into her. He slid them in and out, still kissing her breasts and nipples, and then her mouth, and suddenly she stiffened and cried out into his mouth as he felt her body go taut. Then she bucked and writhed beneath his hand.

Before her spasms could subside he straddled her, pressed the tip of his penis to her vagina, and slid into her wetness.

First she opened her legs wide to receive him, and then she closed them around him. She wrapped her arms around him, as well, and he rode her that way for a long time until finally he withdrew and turned her over. He entered her vagina that way and rode her again. She gasped and got up on her hands and knees and began leaning back into him every time he thrust into her. After a few moments they were both grunting with the effort, pushing toward each other. She was small, but she was strong and met his every thrust until he grasped her hips and groaned loudly as he emptied himself into her. . . .

FORTY-ONE

"Yes," she said later, as they lay together in the bed, "that is what I wanted."

"Good," he said. "I'm glad I could give you what you wanted."

"Now if I died tomorrow," she said, "it would be all right."

"What are you talking about?" he asked. "It wouldn't be all right with me."

She snuggled up closer to him.

"I would like to stay right here, just like this," she said.

"For how long?"

"Forever."

He laughed and squeezed her tightly.

"Then we'd both die . . . of hunger."

At that moment her stomach made a sound that gave away the fact that she was hungry.

"I heard that."

She put her hands over her stomach, as if that would stop the noise.

"That's not going to work," he said. "The only thing that will quiet that is food. Come on, let's go eat."

"Where?"

He released her and rolled away from her to the other side of the bed, where he sat.

"The dining room."

She pulled the sheet up to her chin.

"I cannot."

"You can," he said, "and you will. Now come on. Get dressed and let's go eat."

"They will not let me in."

"They won't turn you away while you're with me."

"Are you sure?"

He smiled at her.

"I'm positive." He stood up and began to dress. "Well, come on."

They were not turned away, but neither were they welcomed with open arms. In fact, as Clint and Jean walked across the dining room floor to a table, Clint knew they were drawing looks for two reasons. One, because people recognized him, and two, because she was Chinese.

As they sat, he saw heads move together as the other diners talked about them. Eventually, the waiter came over to take their order.

"Sir?"

"Shall I order for both of us?" Clint asked her.

"Yes."

"Two steaks, with whatever vegetables you have." He looked at Jean. "Do you drink coffee?"

"Yes."

"A big pot of coffee and two cups."

The waiter looked at Jean as if she was something he had stepped in, then looked at Clint and said, "Very well, sir."

The desk clerk had followed their progress as soon as they had appeared on the stairs, all the way across the lobby to the dining room, and now he was peering at them from the lobby, with just his head showing.

"Everyone is looking at us," Jean said. "I should leave."

"They're looking at me because I killed three men the other night, Jean."

"You cannot fool me," she said. "They are looking at both of us."

"So what?" he asked. "The food is still going to taste good, isn't it?"

"I should not eat here."

"Why not?"

"My people are not eating this well."

"They can eat better with the money they'll be making at the mine, starting tomorrow."

"That is what I came to talk to you about."

"Oh?" he said. "You mean it wasn't only . . ."

She blushed and looked away for a moment, then looked back at him. "I am worried."

"About tomorrow?"

She nodded.

"Have you told your father and uncle that you're worried?"

"Yes."

"And what did they have to say?"

"That our people must work."

"Are your father and uncle going into the mines tomorrow?"

"No," she said. "They are the elders."

"They didn't look that old to me."

"Not old," she said, "but they are the elders."

"I see."

"They will stay behind."

"Who is choosing which of your people goes into the mines?"

"My uncle and father."

"And have they chosen you?"

"Yes," she said, "but I chose myself first."

Suddenly the waiter appeared. He set Clint's plate in front of him, then hastily dropped Jean's so hard that Clint was surprised it didn't break. As it was, some of the vegetables fell off the plate onto the table.

As the waiter started away Clint snapped, "Hey!"

"Sir?"

"Clean that up."

The waiter looked surprised.

"Clint—" Jean started.

"Sir?" the waiter asked.

"I said clean up the mess you made, and while you're at it, apologize for it."

"But, sir, she's—"

"A customer," Clint said. "She's dining here as my guest, and she'll be treated with respect. Do you understand me?"

Clint caught the waiter's eyes and glared at the man until he lowered them. Hastily, the waiter picked up the vegetables that had fallen from the plate. He stood there with them in his hands, not knowing what to do with them.

"Now the apology."

"I'm . . . sorry, ma'am, for the mess."

"It is all right."

"Now bring her some fresh vegetables," Clint said. "A plate of them, and I'd better not hear the plate touch the table."

"Y-yes, sir."

As the waiter walked away, Jean said, "You frightened him."

"I meant to."

"There is no need for you to do this for me."

"Never mind," Clint said. "You just eat that steak and tell me what it was you wanted to tell me."

She looked down at the steak and asked, "May I tell you after we've eaten?"

He laughed and said, "Of course. Dig in."

And she did.

FORTY-TWO

Jean polished off her lunch in half the time it took Clint. In fact, he even gave her the end of his steak, which she ate with the extra vegetables the waiter had brought and set down gently on the table.

Clint was about to order another pot of coffee when he saw Sheriff Reasoner standing in the doorway of the dining room, beckoning to him frantically.

"Jean? Keep eating, I'll be right back."

"Where are you going?"

"Just into the lobby for a few minutes," he said. "I'll be right back."

She popped a potato into her mouth and nodded.

Clint stood up and walked out into the lobby, where the sheriff was waiting impatiently.

"What is it, Sheriff?" Clint asked. "Something happen at the jail?"

"No, Adams, something is happening right here."

"Like what?"

"What do you think you're doing?"

"I'm having lunch."

"I mean, what do you think you're doing bringing her here?" Reasoner demanded.

"She's having lunch, too, with me. She's my guest, Sheriff. Why, is that a problem?"

"The Chinese don't eat where the white folks eat,

157

Adams,'' Reasoner said, lowering his voice. "It just isn't done.''

Clint looked over at the clerk, who was standing behind the counter. The man suddenly found some work to do. Clint was certain that it was he who had sent for the law.

"Are you telling me it's against the law for that young lady to have lunch with me?''

"No,'' Reasoner said, "it ain't against the law, but it just ain't done.''

"Why not?''

"These are respectable people,'' the lawman said. "God-fearing people.''

"And she's not?''

Reasoner lowered his voice again.

"I don't even think they believe in God,'' he said.

"Well,'' Clint said, "she probably believes in her God just as much as you believe in yours.''

Reasoner looked at him like he'd gone crazy.

"There's only one God,'' he said.

"I'm not going to stand here and discuss religion with you, Sheriff,'' Clint said. "What do you want me to do?''

"Get her out of here!''

"Sure,'' Clint said, and the sheriff looked to heave a sigh of relief, until Clint added, "as soon as she's finished eating.''

"No,'' Reasoner said, "now!''

Clint gave the sheriff a hard look.

"And if I don't?''

"If you don't?''

"That's right,'' Clint said. "What will you do if I don't, Sheriff?''

"You—I—'' the lawman stammered. "You're gonna start a riot in here.''

"There's not going to be a riot in here, Sheriff,'' Clint

said. "Not over a steak and a few potatoes. If you're worried about a riot, you'd better worry about it tomorrow, at the mine."

"Adams—"

"I'd think you'd have better things to do with your time than worry about who's eating lunch in the hotel dining room."

"Yeah, but—"

"I'm going back inside to finish my meal," Clint said. "If you want me to leave with that girl before I'm ready, you're going to have to come in and make me."

"But I—"

Clint didn't let the man finish. He turned on his heel, walked back into the dining room, and sat down.

"Is something wrong?" Jean asked.

Clint looked into the lobby where the sheriff seemed to be saying something to the clerk before he turned and stalked out of the hotel.

"No," Clint said, "nothing's wrong at all."

FORTY-THREE

After lunch they went out onto the street and walked while they talked.

"Aren't you worried about your people?" Clint asked.

"Yes, I am."

"Well, you know," Clint said, "maybe there won't be a strike. Then your people won't be in danger of getting hurt."

"And they will not be working either," she said. "They would rather risk the danger and work."

"I see. Why did you come to see me, Jean?"

"I thought . . . maybe you would be there tomorrow," she said. "People fear you."

"You think my presence will keep the miners from rioting?"

"I hoped . . ."

"I don't think so, Jean," he said, "but if it helps you at all, I already intend to be there. In fact, I'm still going to work on averting a strike all day."

"Averting," she said, "means avoiding?"

"Yes."

She stopped walking.

"That is not what I want. I told you, my people want to work."

"Well," he said, "even if there's no strike Craig might hire some of you."

"Not enough," she said, "not nearly enough. Please, you must not . . . avert?"

"Jean," Clint said, "I don't know what to do that would be right for everyone."

"Just let us work," she said, "that is all. I must go back now."

"All right."

"Thank you for . . . well, for everything."

He smiled.

"Thank you, too," he said. "I'll see you tomorrow, at the mine."

"Yes," she said, "at the mine."

He watched her walk away and noticed that other people were watching her walk away, too. He was sure, though, that they were not thinking the same thing he was.

When she was out of sight he turned and walked back to his hotel. Instead of going inside he grabbed a wooden chair that was outside and sat down on it, leaning back against the wall so that the front two legs were off the ground.

Heading the strike off would certainly avoid a riot, but it would also assure that most of Jean's people remained out of work. He wondered if there were other jobs they could get in town. But from the way people had looked at her, he doubted anyone would hire her, or any other Chinese. No, the only chance the Chinese had was to work the mines, if they could do so without getting slaughtered by the striking miners.

And what were the chances of that?

FORTY-FOUR

Clint knew he didn't have time to talk to as many of the miners as it might take to avoid the strike. His only chance was to talk directly to Mike Garrett, if the man would talk to him.

He had dinner alone in the hotel dining room. He was still drawing looks from the man who had waited on him and Jean that morning. Those looks were a mixture of fear and annoyance. However, the man's performance was perfect. He never spilled one drop or banged one plate down.

Over dinner Clint thought about Virginia and Jean. He wondered if he and Virginia would ever speak again after what had happened the last time he saw her. Did he want to speak to her? Probably just to say good-bye, but nothing more.

As for Jean, he was now worried that she'd end up getting hurt when she and her people arrived at the mines in the morning. The only way to keep that from happening was to try to avert a strike or, in the absence of that, avoid a riot.

He wondered if one man with a gun would be able to put down a riot. He'd never tried it before, but he had stood off lynch mobs in his days as a lawman, and they sometimes numbered as many as a hundred people.

This, however, was going to be a much larger group.

He wondered if the sheriff would actually be there tomorrow, with or without some reluctant deputies. If he
had to bet on Reasoner, he'd bet that the man wouldn't
be there.

That would leave him to watch, probably helplessly,
as things escalated . . . unless he could do some good
tonight by finding and talking to Mike Garrett.

He finished dinner and decided to try the saloon.

The saloon looked as if it was more than half filled
with miners, the rest of the customers being townspeople. Clint got himself a beer and didn't see Garrett at
the bar. Beer in hand he began to walk around the
crowded saloon, seeking the man out. He finally found
him, but Garrett was involved in a poker game. Clint
didn't want to interrupt him, but there was a chair open
at the table, which would give him a perfect place to
watch Garrett from.

"Mind if I sit in?" he asked, standing by the empty
chair.

Garrett looked up from his cards and saw Clint standing there.

"Naw, I don't mind," he said. "Anybody else
mind?"

Nobody did and Clint sat down and placed his beer
on the table. It was unusual for him to have a beer while
playing poker, but in this instance the beer had come
first. Once that one was gone, he would not be having
another.

Clint watched as the hand played itself out and Garrett
took it with two pair.

As the cards were gathered by the new dealer, the man
explained the game to Clint.

"Five-card draw is all we're playing," the dealer said.
"Quarter and a half, a dollar raise limit."

"Fine," Clint said.

The dealer nodded, shuffled, and dealt out five cards to the six players. With Garrett right across from him, Clint was free to concentrate on his cards without losing track of the man.

He picked his cards up off the table when all five were dealt. Clint noticed that three of the six men picked their cards up one at a time as they were dealt to them. More experienced players usually waited until all five cards were dealt, so this told him that at least three of the players were inexperienced—or simply less experienced—to some degree.

Clint fanned his cards out in his hand and stared at them. He couldn't remember the last time he'd been dealt a full house, but there it was, pretty as you please, three queens and two tens.

The man to his right was the first bettor and he bet a quarter. Clint, not knowing how these men would respond to an early raise, simply called. Luckily the next player raised a quarter, and the one after him raised a half. When the bet got to Mike Garrett he called, as did the dealer, and he opened.

"Another raise," Clint said, upping it another half dollar.

The man who had raised initially frowned, thought a moment, then called.

The second raiser went another half, and everyone at the table called. Clint wondered at the fact that no one folded. He wondered if he was at a table filled with players who never folded. If he was, he wasn't going to enjoy this game, because such players made any sort of strategy a waste of time. A player who won't fold changes the entire complexion of the game, and a table full of them would simply ruin it.

Clint decided to see right away if that's what he was in for.

"Cards?" the dealer asked.

The opener took three.

Clint said, ''I'll play these.''

''One,'' said the first raiser.

''I'll stay pat,'' the second raiser said.

''Jeez,'' the next man said. ''Two pat hands, what am I doin' in this hand?'' But he took two cards.

''One,'' Mike Garrett said.

''I'm gonna fold, gents,'' the dealer said, ''so I can just concentrate on the deal.''

The opener drew three.

At last, Clint thought, somebody had folded.

Now, he thought, let's see how the rest of the hand goes.

FORTY-FIVE

The opener checked to Clint, who said, "Bet a dollar."

The next man folded, renewing Clint's faith in humanity.

"Raise," the other pat hand said, chipping in another dollar.

"Fold," said the next man.

"Call," said Mike Garrett. Staying in against two pat hands but not raising. Clint wondered what Garrett could have.

The dealer had already folded, so the bet went to the opener.

"Fold."

Clint said, "Your dollar, and another."

The man with the other pat hand leaned forward and said, "Why don't we raise the stakes? Anybody object?"

It was only he, Clint, and Mike Garrett in the game, so it fell to them to answer.

"I don't have a problem with that."

"Me neither," Garrett said.

"Fine," the man said, "then I raise—"

"But you're folding," Clint said, interrupting the man.

"What?"

Clint smiled at him.

"You're folding."

"Why would I do that?" the man asked.

"Because he," Clint said, indicating the dealer, "dealt you a pat hand."

"He dealt you one, too," the man said. "So what?"

"But I'll bet yours is bigger than mine."

"So?" the man said again. "That's what the game's about."

"I'll bet you have kings full," Clint said.

"What are you saying?" Garrett asked.

Clint looked at him.

"And I'll bet you have jacks full."

Garrett sat back, a surprised look on his face.

"See," Clint said, indicating the dealer again, "he knows exactly what he's doing. He dealt me a pat hand, his partner a pat hand, and he filled you in when you drew one card. Then his partner decides it's time to up the stakes. Since we're both sitting here with full houses, we agree to it. See?"

"You mean . . . they're cheatin'?" Garrett demanded.

"That's exactly what I mean."

"Mister," the man with the other pat hand said, "you better be kiddin'."

Clint looked at the dealer, who was sweating.

"You," he said, and the dealer jumped, startled.

"Y-yes?"

"You've got a choice," he said. "You can back his play, or you can get up and walk out of here now."

"I—I—I got money on the table."

"Leave it."

"But—"

"Five seconds to make up your mind."

The count was three when the man pushed his chair back and got up.

"You son of a—"

"Quiet!" Clint snapped. "You get to make the next decision."

The dealer hurriedly left the room, which had become quiet. Their table had become the center of attention as soon as the word "cheat" had been heard.

"Now it's your turn," Clint said to the other man. "Get up and leave."

"I ain't leavin' without my money."

"Yes, you are."

"Mister," he said, "I got a gun on you under the table."

In fact, both of the man's hands were out of sight beneath the table.

"Is that right?"

"Yeah, that is right," the man said. "Now, I ain't leavin' without my money, so I suggest you either play the hand out or you leave."

Clint stared at the man.

"If you've got a gun on me under the table," Clint said, "you'd better use it."

He heard people scrambling to get out of the line of fire.

"Mister," Garrett said to the man, "I think you picked the wrong man to try to cheat."

"Whataya mean?" the man asked.

"Do you know who that is?" Garrett asked, indicating Clint.

The man hesitated, then said, "No."

"That's Clint Adams, friend," Garrett said, "the wrong man to try to cheat."

"Adams?" The man turned his eyes to Clint. "The Gunsmith?"

"Like I said," Clint said, "use the gun or walk out. You've got the same five seconds your friend had."

"Wait a minute . . ."

"One . . ."

"Uh, look . . ."

"Two . . ."

"All right, all right!" the man said, and pulled his hands out from under the table—empty. "I'm going."

"And keep going," Clint said. "Don't let me see you or your friend in town tomorrow. Understand?"

"Yeah, sure," the man said, sliding his chair back so hastily that it fell over, "I understand." He tripped over the chair, almost fell, and then ran for the door.

Clint looked at Garrett.

"You got any objection to splitting this pot evenly among everyone at the table?"

"Nope," Garrett said, "no objection at all."

With the other two men gone, the remaining four came out ahead, anyway, after they split the pot.

"That's it for me," one of them said.

"Me, too," another said.

Clint said, "This was the shortest game I ever played in." He looked at Garrett. "Buy you a drink?"

"You saved me some money," Garrett said. "I think I should buy you one."

"Why not?"

FORTY-SIX

Clint and Garrett managed to find a table in the back and took their beers there. A couple of saloon girls came over, but they shooed them away.

"Let's talk strike, Mike."

Garrett shook his head and said, "Craig ain't gonna change his mind, Adams—"

"Why don't you call me Clint?"

"I'll call you Clint," Garrett said, "but it ain't gonna change anything."

"I saved you some money, you said, so maybe you owe me a few minutes of listening?"

Garrett firmed his jaw for a moment, then said, "Okay, go ahead."

"The men will listen to you if you tell them not to strike."

"No, they won't," Garrett said.

"But you speak for them."

"I just told you and Craig what they wanted me to tell you," Garrett said. "I don't control them."

"Mike, what's going to happen tomorrow morning when the Chinese Craig hired to work in your place show up?"

"That's easy," Garrett said, "you're gonna have some dead Chinese."

"Is that how you want to play it?"

"Not me," Garrett said, "but the others will. I ain't the violent type."

"You're not?"

Garrett was surprised at Clint's surprise.

"I'm a big guy, Clint, and I don't let nobody push me around, but I ain't violent. Why? Who told you I was?"

Clint decided to tell him the truth.

"Virginia."

"What?" Garrett exploded. "I never laid a hand on her. Did she say I did?"

"No, but she said she believed you would. She said if she had left Sam for you, sooner or later you would have hit her."

"I ain't never hit a woman," Garrett said. "Why would she say something like that?"

"I don't know," Clint said. "Why don't we ask her?"

They left the saloon and walked over to Virginia's house. They were approaching it when there was a shot. Garrett grunted, stumbled, and fell. Clint turned quickly, drawing his gun. He was in time to see the muzzle flash in the dark, and then the bullet struck him. It must have hit him in the head, because suddenly it was dark, and he was falling. As he fell he pulled the trigger of his gun as many times as he could before he went numb. . . .

FORTY-SEVEN

"What happened?"

The words were out even before he realized he was conscious, and alive.

He was lying on his back, looking up at Sheriff Reasoner.

"Doc says you got lucky," Reasoner said. "The bullet creased your scalp."

Clint turned his head and saw another man in the room, probably the doctor.

"What about Garrett?" he asked.

"He wasn't as lucky," the doctor said. "Shot in the back, killed instantly."

"Damn," Clint said, closing his eyes. His head was pounding.

"He's over at the undertaker's," Reasoner said. "Do you remember what happened?"

"I don't—I'm not sure. Let me think a minute."

Clint closed his eyes and tried to re-create the incidents of . . . of when?

"How long have I been out?" he asked.

"Most of the night. Somebody found the two of you in the street and called for me."

"Virginia?"

"What about her?"

"We were in front of her house," Clint said. "She

must have heard the shots. Didn't she send for you?"

Reasoner shook his head.

"I haven't seen her."

"Can I sit up?"

"Sure," the doctor said, "but slowly."

Reasoner helped Clint sit up, and the pounding in his head got worse. He touched it, felt a bandage around his head like a turban.

"Do you remember what happened?" Reasoner asked.

"We were on our way to talk to Virginia," Clint said. "We were approaching her house when I heard a shot. Garrett stumbled and went down. I turned, saw the muzzle flash, and that's it. I'm surprised I'm still alive."

"You heard two shots," Reasoner said. "The fella who found you said he heard five or six. Your gun's empty. My guess is you were pulling the trigger as you went down, and scared the guy off. Or maybe—yeah, maybe he thought he got you. Maybe he thinks you're dead."

"I can't believe Virginia didn't hear the shots and come out," Clint said.

"Maybe she wasn't home," Reasoner said.

"Or maybe she just didn't want to," Clint said.

"What do you mean?"

"I mean maybe I've been going about this all wrong," Clint said.

"Going about what?"

"Looking into Sam's death," Clint said. "All along both Virginia and Craig have been denying that they were involved."

"And you think they were?"

"It would answer a lot of questions if they were," Clint said. "We should talk to both of them."

"I was gonna go over to the mine this morning," Reasoner said.

"Jesus," Clint said, "the mine. What time is it?"

"Almost nine," the sheriff said.

"We might already be too late."

He got off the table he'd been lying on.

"Take it easy, Mr. Adams," the doc said.

Clint leaned on Reasoner.

"We've got to go."

"All right. Come on."

They went to the front door and walked outside. Suddenly, as if from far off, they heard the sound of shots—lots of shots.

"I think you're right," Reasoner said. "I think we're too late."

FORTY-EIGHT

There was no way to stop it. By the time Clint and the sheriff got there the riot was in full swing. Clint found out later that the miners had congregated in front of Jeff Banks's shack, demanding to know what Rod Craig had decided. When Banks told them that Craig wasn't going to give in to their demands they set fire to the shack. They were a mob by the time the Chinese workers arrived, and that's all it took. Some of them had guns and started shooting right away. The Chinese had no weapons, so they were helpless to do anything but run—but the miners wouldn't let it go at that. With a lynch mob mentality they chased the Chinese, shot some of them, killed others with shovels and pickaxes. It was a bloodbath by the time Clint and Reasoner reached the scene, and they were helpless to do anything.

There were people running everywhere, miners chasing the Chinese workers, running them down, shooting at them or fighting with them. Clint thought once or twice he should use his gun, but on who? He looked to his right and saw Jeff Banks standing off to the side, the burning shack behind him. The man was hatless, bleeding from the head, a bewildered look on his face. Apparently the men had pulled him from the shack and clubbed him before setting fire to it.

Clint walked over to where Banks was.

"I couldn't stop them," Banks said.

"No one could," Clint said.

Already the crowd was starting to thin out as the Chinese ran off with the miners in pursuit. There were bloodied bodies lying on the ground, some unmoving, some groaning and clutching their wounds.

"I got something to tell you," Banks said. "About Craig, and Virginia, and about . . . Sam Crider's death."

"It's a little late, Banks."

"I know," Banks said, "but I got to tell you . . . I got to . . ."

Twenty-eight Chinese workers were killed that day, fifteen more wounded, and hundreds of them were driven from town in what went down in history as the Rock Springs Massacre. Clint couldn't help but feel that he might have prevented it if he'd been there earlier, or if he'd connected Virginia Madison and Rod Craig sooner than he did.

"Oh, my God," was what Reasoner had said when they reached the scene.

Clint could only nod his head in agreement.

"What do I do?" Reasoner asked later.

They were in his office, he and Clint. They had collected some of the townspeople to help get the bodies picked up. The doctor was treating the injured Chinese, and a few miners who'd managed to injure themselves by trampling each other.

"You need to call in some federal help," Clint said. "Those miners are going to have to be arrested, and you're going to need marshals to do that."

Clint's head was still pounding. His hat was on the sheriff's desk because it hurt too much to put it on his head. The sheriff sat behind his desk, a dazed look on his face.

"I ain't never seen anything like it," he said.

"Lynch mob mentality," Clint said. "If you want to stay a sheriff you're going to deal with it a lot more, probably on a smaller scale, though."

"This fella I got in the cell," Reasoner said. "He turned out to be pretty lucky. I thought they might come for him, but this turned out to be the safest place for him."

"I guess so."

"What happened to that girl you know?" Reasoner asked. "The one who wanted to bring this one some food?"

"Jean."

"Yeah . . . was she among the dead?"

"There was one woman killed," Clint said, "the rest were men. It wasn't her. She wasn't among the wounded either. I don't know where she is."

"Maybe you should go look for her?"

"Maybe," Clint said, "but first I've got to find Virginia and Craig."

"You really think they killed Crider?"

"I talked to Jeff Banks," Clint said. "He says they did."

"You believe him?"

"I do," Clint said.

"Why?"

"Same reason I believed him," he said, inclining his head toward the cells.

"What'd he say?"

"Apparently Virginia felt him out a while ago about killing Sam."

"She asked him to?"

"Not in so many words," Clint said, "but he's sure that's what she meant."

"Why didn't Banks come to me?"

"He didn't want to lose his job," Clint said. "See,

Banks knew that Craig and Virginia were seeing each other. He didn't want to say anything, though. He's always been Craig's man.''

"So why talk now? To you?"

"Because he knows it's all over."

"And who's been trying to kill you all along?" Reasoner asked. "Who killed Garrett and tried to get you last night?"

"Banks says Craig has a man working for him. He's on the payroll, but he's not a miner."

"A gunman?"

"Probably."

"A hired killer in my town?"

"Maybe not anymore."

"Whataya mean?"

"I think everything blew up in everyone's faces this morning," Clint said. "I think Craig really didn't think the miners would do what they did this morning. In fact, I'll bet the miners didn't think this would happen."

"It got out of hand."

"Oh, yes," Clint said, "it did."

"Did Banks tell you this gunman's name?"

"Rankin," Clint said, "Ian Rankin."

"You ever hear of him?"

"No."

"You gonna go after him?"

"No," Clint said. "He was doin' his job, doin' what he was paid to do."

"By Craig."

"Yes, and that's who I want to see, Craig, and Virginia."

"With me along?"

"That would help."

Reasoner handed Clint his hat.

"Let's go find 'em."

Clint took the hat but didn't put it on his head.

Watch for

CRIMINAL KIN

195th novel in the exciting GUNSMITH series
from JOVE

Coming in April!